da

Down
the
WICKET

THE GLORY GARDENS SERIES
(in suggested reading order)

Down the WICKET

BOB CATTELL

· · · · · · · · · · · · · · · · ·

Illustrations by
David Kearney

RED FOX

Published by Random House Children's Books
61-63 Uxbridge Road, London, W5 5SA

Addresses for companies within The Random House Group Limited can be
found at: www.randomhouse.co.uk/offices.htm

12

The Random House Group Limited supports the Forest Stewardship
Council (FSC®), the leading international forest certification organisation.
Our books carrying the FSC label are printed on FSC® certified paper. FSC
is the only forest certification scheme endorsed by the leading environmental
organisations, including Greenpeace. Our paper procurement policy can be
found at www.randomhouse.co.uk/environment

Set in Sabon by SX Composing DTP, Rayleigh, Essex

Printed and bound by CPI Group (UK) Ltd, Croydon, CR0 4YY

The Random House Group Limited Reg. No. 954009

www.kidsatrandomhouse.co.uk

A Red Fox Book
978 0 099 40903 8

Contents

Chapter One

There's nothing like the beginning of the cricket season for dreams. You can do anything, be anything – score the fastest hundred, take a hat trick in your first over, win the League. A golden summer lies before you.

I was standing in the middle of the square at the Eastgate Priory cricket pitch, looking at the wicket and dreaming. It was Glory Gardens' first pre-season net practice and I'd arrived early. No one else was around and I began to think about our first League game against Croyland Crusaders, which was less than two weeks away.

Even I had to admit that we would struggle to improve on last year's amazing results. Glory Gardens had won everything in sight: the under 13s League; the national Champions League against the best teams in the country, and to round things off nicely we'd just returned from a triumphant tour of Barbados. A year ago no one had heard of Glory Gardens C.C.; now we are one of the most famous junior cricket teams in the land. Everyone is looking forward to the new season and, after the West Indies tour, we are all match fit, apart from Frankie, who thinks a training diet is seeing how many burgers he can eat between meals.

I walked back from the end of the square and measured out my 15-pace run up. Then I raced in and bowled an imaginary off-cutter. In my mind's eye I saw the ball bounce on a perfect length, cut back sharply between the batsman's bat and pad and rip out the middle stump. As it cartwheeled through the air and the bails flew, I swung round, arm raised in triumph, and on one knee screamed an appeal at the nonexistent umpire. That was when I saw Frankie and Cal walking towards me from the pavilion, pointing.

"If the first sign of madness is talking to yourself, what does playing cricket on your own without a bat and ball make you?" said Frankie to Cal in a loud voice. Frankie is Glory Gardens' plump wicket-keeper, and Cal usually opens the batting and bowls handy off-breaks – he lives next door to me and he's my best friend. I'm Hooker Knight, by the way, captain of Glory Gardens. My nickname 'Hooker' comes from my initials: Harry Oliver O'Neil Knight.

"So this is what the captain gets up to when he's on his own," said Cal with a grin. "How many wickets have you bagged so far, Hooker?" Being captain doesn't protect you from the teasing – especially in the company of Frankie and Cal.

"Have you seen Kiddo yet?" asked Frankie.

"No. He's not here."

"Isn't he the one who's always moaning about us not being on time for nets?" said Frankie. It was true enough. Kiddo Johnstone, our coach, is usually a stickler for punctuality.

Kiddo opens the batting for Eastgate Priory First XI. He was a county cricket pro when he was younger but now he's our French teacher – Frankie calls it a sad case of a career in free fall. No one understands the game better than Kiddo; his training methods have played a big part in turning Glory Gardens from a team of hopefuls and no-hopers into champions.

"We'd better get changed and start without him," I said, spotting some of the others arriving at the pavilion.

It was a warm and sunny April day and Frankie's sister, Jo, the team secretary and organiser of everything that happens at the club, got us together for a photo before training started. As usual Clive was the last to arrive. Jo put her camera on

8

automatic and joined the group. That's her on the right. Frankie is the one wearing wicket-keeper's pads in the front row. Ohbert – sitting between them with his Walkman on full blast – is our secret weapon. He looks like the worst cricketer in the world but he has the habit of making strange things happen on the cricket field, usually by accident or sheer fluke. No one who saw it will ever forget his amazing run-out in the League of Champions final or the boundary catch against Griffiths Hall in Barbados.

Back row: Marty Lear, Erica Davies,
Cal Sebastien, Tylan Vellacott, Matthew Rose,
Kris Johansen, Clive da Costa
Front row: Azzie Nazar, Mack McCurdy,
Jacky Gunn, Hooker Knight, Frankie Allen,
Ohbert Bennett, Jo Allen

If Ohbert is at one end of Glory Gardens' rainbow of talent, then way out at the other are Clive and Azzie, probably the best two bats in the county, and Marty, who is a deadly fast bowler. This is how the squad's specialist skills break down:

Batters	Clive, Azzie, Matthew, Mack
Seam bowlers	Marty, Jacky, Kris
Spin bowler	Tylan
All-rounders	Hooker, Erica, Cal
Wicket-keeper	Frankie
No. 11 bat	Ohbert

I usually bat at five or six and come on as first change bowler after Marty and Jacky – I bowl left arm, medium-fast. Erica is a brilliant containing bowler and an excellent middle order bat.

There was still no sign of Kiddo, so I started to organise things. I split the players into two groups. Cal and Matthew put on their pads and went into the nets with Erica, Marty, Jacky, Tylan and Kris bowling at them. The rest of us concentrated on fielding practice in the deep, using the plan Kiddo had taught us.

Mack is Glory Gardens' outstanding fielder; his ability to pick up the ball on the run – sliding, collecting and throwing all in one movement – can be breathtaking. His throw is deadly accurate too and his speed and aggression in the covers is usually worth a wicket or ten runs every game.

Ohbert had been watching Mack's sliding stops and it wasn't long before he was ready to try one of his own. The ball he chose to attack was bouncing towards him quite fast when, to everyone's horror, he launched himself at it with a violent two-footed sliding tackle. Both feet shot up in the air and he was almost standing on his head when the ball struck him square on the bum and he rolled back on top of it with a loud grunt.

"Nice one, Ohbert," shouted Frankie. "But you're supposed to get behind the ball – not get the ball on the behind."

Azzie helped a gasping Ohbert to his feet, and we were still laughing when Kiddo appeared. Something about his expression brought everyone to their senses.

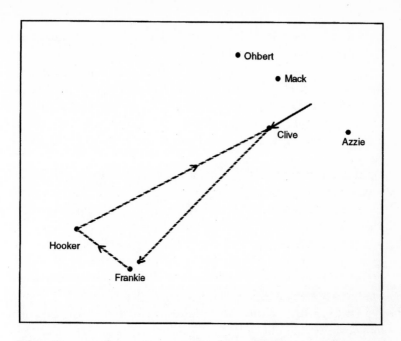

This is a good way to practise long distance catching and fielding skills and it tests the accuracy of your throwing in to the keeper too. Frankie stands by a single stump with me alongside him. I knock the ball one-handed, using an old bat, either in the air or along the ground to the arc of fielders. The nearest fielder races in and catches or picks it up on the run and immediately throws in over the stump to Frankie, who chucks the ball to me, and so on.

He called us all together and we sat on the grass in a circle round him. Old Gatting, Kiddo's fat, wheezy mongrel, waddled over too and picked out Ohbert to sit next to. Perhaps he shares his taste in music – if so, he's the only one.

"I've got some bad news about the Priory, kiddoes," Kiddo said grimly. Glory Gardens is the junior team of the Eastgate Priory club, which puts out three senior League teams too.

"Is that why you're late for nets?" asked Frankie.

Kiddo ignored him. "I've been on the phone to our landlords," he continued, "and they've just told me that we've lost the Priory ground."

"Sounds a bit careless," said Frankie, who can't remain serious for two seconds, especially when everyone would prefer him to shut up. Jo gave him a fierce dig in the ribs.

"They've sold it," continued Kiddo. "The entire ground is going to be developed as a superstore and restaurant complex."

"But there are loads of supermarkets . . ." began Jo.

Kiddo sighed. "I know, kiddo. And you don't have to tell me either that there *aren't* loads of cricket pitches. It's a big blow and no mistake. With luck and some good fixture planning Eastgate Priory First XI might be able to play its games over at the Groves. But there's no room there for the other teams. Heaven knows where the seconds, thirds and you lot are going to play this season."

"This season!" said Cal. "You mean they're throwing us out now?"

"From today. We don't even get a week's notice," said Kiddo, grimly.

"That's impossible," said Jo. "Our season starts a week on Wednesday."

"I undestand how you feel," said Kiddo. "But I'm afraid there's nothing we can do. They've been planning this for some time and keeping it all very quiet. I imagine they're hoping the new building will go up quickly and, after a bit, everyone will just come to accept it as part of the scenery."

"Oh no they won't," said Frankie, suddenly jumping to his feet and looking as fierce as someone Frankie's shape can. "We'll fight them for it. They can't just . . ."

"They can, Frankie," Kiddo said solemnly. "They've got everything on their side: the money, the council, the law. No one is going to let a little cricket club stand in the way of a multimillion-pound development."

"We'll start a protest; barricade the gates," said Mack.

"Yeah, and we can pack the pavilion with booby traps and chain ourselves up in the oak tree," said Frankie.

Kiddo smiled. "Somehow I don't see you as an eco-warrior, Frankie. But I know how you feel. A lot of people have worked hard for this club, including you lot, and it's sad to see it come to an end. We're launching an appeal to the Sports Minister but I don't suppose much will come of that. In the meantime, we have no right to play here and if Glory Gardens is going to compete in the League this year, you'd better put your energies into finding a new ground."

"Where?" I asked. "There are no cricket pitches round here. The nearest is the Wanderers and that's completely booked up."

"We wouldn't want to play there anyway, we'd catch something nasty," said Frankie. Wyckham Wanderers are one of the top teams in the county and Glory Gardens' deadliest local rivals.

"There is perhaps somewhere," said Jo, looking thoughtful.

"Where?"

"Glory Gardens."

"You don't mean the playing field?" said Cal in disbelief. Glory Gardens C.C. took its name from the recreation ground at the back of Bason Street where Cal and I live. Most of us played there before we formed a proper club and moved to the Priory. But it's not a real cricket ground. It's just a council rec and a lumpy and bumpy one at that – full of rabbit holes and molehills. It's used mainly by joggers and people walking their dogs.

"We can't play there, stupid," scoffed Clive.

"Why not?"

"For a start the pitch is a disgrace, the outfield's like a paddock and it hasn't got a pavilion. Apart from that it's a great idea."

"We could cut the grass and roll the pitch," Jo said stubbornly. "And there is that old gardener's hut that no one uses any more; maybe we could change in that."

"You're crazy," said Clive.

"Has anyone else got a better idea?"

No one spoke.

"Then who's with me?" said Jo. "Who wants to try and get Glory Gardens rec ready for the new season?"

Matthew's hand shot up immediately, followed by Cal, Tylan and Azzie. I looked at Cal and shrugged and then raised mine too, and slowly, one by one, more hands went up until the majority were behind Jo's plan. But Clive and Marty refused to budge. As Marty put it, "We're a good club now and we could be even better, but not if we play on a rubbish pitch."

Frankie wouldn't support his sister either. "I say we stay at the Priory and fight to the death," he cried. "All for one and one for all. Who's with me?"

Ohbert, who had raised his hand with the rest of us without hearing a word of the discussion, suddenly jumped to his feet and took off his headset. "Oh . . . but I will . . . I'll fight with you, Frankie."

Frankie looked at the others. "So it's just you and me then, Ohbert. We'll show them. We'll keep our cricket ground because we're not going to be pushed around by some miserable supermarket chain."

But we all knew, Frankie better than anyone, that there was little point in arguing with Jo when her mind was made up. She was already discussing her plans with Kiddo, and after nets everyone, including the doubters, went over to Glory Gardens' rec to take a proper look at the place.

Chapter Two

The next week was madly busy. Thanks to Jo, things happened fast at the rec, and finally it began to look as if the first League game on Wednesday evening against Croyland Crusaders would go ahead after all.

At first sight, though, the ground had appeared a disaster. We had all walked round gloomily, prodding the pitch and peering through the cobwebby window of the little gardener's shed, which was full of junk almost to its roof. The outfield was as bad as Clive had said. The long grass was matted and tangled and there were loads of molehills dotted around. But the biggest problem was the playing area itself. There are two old cricket pitches in the middle of the playing field, which were last used for matches about two or three years ago. Since then the strips have become overgrown with weeds and the surface bumpy and cracked. There was even a molehill on a length at one end, which Frankie said would help Cal to turn his off-breaks for the first time ever.

But Jo wasn't put off by the general gloom. Within a couple of days she'd got permission from the council to use the ground for matches and training. Kiddo arranged for Bunter, the Priory groundsman, to come over with his mower and heavy roller, and after a couple of cuts the outfield didn't look too bad, though there was a nasty boggy patch down the slope at the Hereward Road end near the ditch. Even the pitches looked flatter and firmer after a few days hard work.

15

On Saturday we gave training a miss, apart from a few overs in the nets which Bunter had erected under the trees. Instead we tackled the job of clearing all the rubbish from the old gardener's shed into a skip which Tylan's dad had had delivered. Mr Vellacott and Kiddo supervised the job but we did most of the work. Predictably Clive didn't turn up, and neither did Frankie or Ohbert. Marty grumbled and groaned throughout the morning but no one took any notice of him – Marty and gloom go together like bangers and mash; Frankie says he's one of those people who always expects his toast to land with the butter-side face down.

The shed looked bigger once we'd thrown all the rubbish out and given it a good clean. You've never seen so much junk; there wasn't a single thing worth keeping. Kiddo brought over some of the benches from the Priory changing rooms and put up clothes hooks. Soon the old shed was beginning to look like a real pavilion changing room, although it was on the small side for two teams to use at once; we'd probably have to come already changed for home games from now on.

By the time Frankie and Ohbert showed up we'd nearly finished the job. Frankie was carrying a roll of posters and Ohbert had a glue bucket and a brush. Kiddo's old dog and club mascot, Gatting, waddled along beside them; he often follows Ohbert about. "We'll put another one up here, Ohbert," said Frankie, and he grabbed the brush, plastered the shed door with glue and stuck a poster right in the middle of it. It read:

**ANOTHER WHITMART? NO. NEVER.
GLORY GARDENS LIVES FOR EVER.**

"What does it mean, Frankie?" asked Cal with a puzzled look.

"What do you think it means, stupid?" said Frankie. "Look! I've got heaps of them here. We've been putting them

16

up all round the Priory. Would you believe it's all boarded up already? There's a big 'sold' sign by the main gate except it's now covered with our posters and we've stuck up loads more round town too, haven't we, Ohbert?" Ohbert grinned foolishly and happily displayed two more rather badly hand-lettered posters:

GLORY GARDENS PLAYERS SHOUT
WE'LL BOWL WHITMART OUT

WHITMART'S CASH IS
CRICKET'S ASHES.

"You'll get arrested putting those up, Francis," said Jo.

"No I won't. Everyone has got a right to protest," insisted Frankie. "And look at this . . . show them, Ohbert." Ohbert grinned again and took his shirt off. Underneath was a white tee-shirt – on the front it said: GLORY GARDENS IN and, on the back, WHITMART OUT.

"Whitmart? That's the supermarket chain, isn't it?" said Matthew.

"Oh, well done, Matt. Ten out of ten for being up-to-date with the news," said Frankie, laying on the sarcasm. "Yes, it's Whitmart that's taking over the Priory. We've just plastered their shop in the High Street with posters."

"Do you think a giant company like that is going to take any notice of you and Ohbert?" said Marty.

"You'd be surprised," said Frankie brightly. "A lot of people came up to us and said they're on our side."

"You mean that traffic warden, Frankie?" said Ohbert.

"And the woman who gave you 50p when you were sitting with Gatting outside the supermarket. I think she thought you were begging."

"You're wasting your time, Frankie," said Cal inspecting one of the posters. "There no chance that anyone will be able to read your writing."

17

"When we win the Priory back you'll be ashamed you said that," said Frankie, and he strode off to stick another poster on a nearby tree.

I helped Kiddo mark out the boundary with white paint. It gave me a chance to talk to him about how the pitch would play on Wednesday and which players to pick. Kiddo said Clive had told him he was thinking of joining another club. "I don't think he really wants to leave Glory Gardens but, now he's been picked for the county, he says he needs to bat regularly on good tracks. He might have a point, I suppose."

"But Azzie's in the county squad too and so am I. Do you think playing at the rec will be bad for our batting?"

"No, kiddo. You've got to learn to bat on every surface – flat tracks and wickets with a bit of life in them too. It won't do you any harm. But Clive hasn't got your confidence. You know what he's like. He tells you how good he is all the time, but a couple of bad scores and he can fall apart for weeks. Don't worry about him. My guess is that he'll come round in the end. Give him time."

"You mean leave him out of the team on Wednesday?"

"You could tell him he's rested this week for missing nets. That's your rule, isn't it?"

"I suppose so. He doesn't know we spent all morning cleaning up the shed instead of practising. But Kris can't play on Wednesday either. She's performing with the school orchestra in some concert."

"So that leaves 11 of you. It doesn't sound as if there's much of a job for the selection committee to do."

It was bad luck that it rained on Wednesday morning. The heavy morning showers stopped Bunter giving the pitch a final cut and roll, and when the sun came out in the afternoon it began to dry.

"Looks like a bowler's paradise," said Cal as we inspected the grassy pitch before the game. "There's nothing worse to

18

bat on than a green, drying wicket, except perhaps a green, drying, bumpy wicket. Just make sure you win the toss."

I lost and Alex Forsyth, their captain, took no time in deciding to put us in.

Matthew and Cal opened the batting as usual. They were both very quiet before they went out. Matthew's always like that, he never says much, but Cal normally tries to joke a bit to relax himself.

The very first ball from Fred Duffield, Crusaders' opening quick bowler, pitched on a length and took off like a scalded cat. Matthew, on strike, snatched the bat out of the way but the ball followed him and grazed his glove. The keeper caught it cleanly and screamed out an appeal. Matthew walked down the pitch, jabbed at it angrily with his bat, and walked back slowly towards the gardener's shed.

Azzie's first ball was a shooter which struck him on the pad and must have been perilously close to lbw. He took the next on his shoulder and the fourth ball of the over popped up from a length and hit him in the face with a nasty *splat* sound that you could hear from the boundary. Azzie went down with blood pouring from his nose but he quickly sat up and, throwing his helmet to one side, wiped away the blood. Eventually the square-leg umpire helped him off the pitch.

"It's not what you'd call friendly out there," said Azzie, slumping down on the bench alongside me as everyone huddled round to see his injury.

"Are you okay? Can you bat later?" I asked.

"Yeah. I'll be fine. It feels like I just walked into Lennox Lewis's fist," mumbled Azzie through the large white handkerchief he was holding over his nose. Frankie went off to get him some ice from Cal's house.

We watched Erica taking guard and then jerk her body out of the path of another vicious lifter. By now no one was looking forward to batting and every ball was greeted with an "Ooh" or an "Aah". Cal and Erica had their hands full keeping shooters out of their stumps or taking evasive action against the throat balls. Predictably, the first runs on the board were four wides, as Cal ducked under another lifter and the keeper failed to get a glove on it. Then he dabbed the next rising ball through the vacant third slip area for two and was clean bowled two balls later by a daisycutter which shot under his bat.

Mack decided that he wasn't going to hang around and wait for the inevitable unplayable ball. He danced down the wicket to the second delivery he received and gave himself room to ping it over cover for a glorious boundary. The next ball cut him in two and missed the off-stump by the width of a coat of varnish.

"Call this cricket?" complained Marty. "How can you have a proper contest on a surface like this."

"I'll just go and put my body armour on," said Frankie, going off to find his pads.

"Crazy game!" said Tylan, adding mysteriously, "the can is open and the worms are on the floor."

"Too right, Ty," said Marty. "We shouldn't be playing League cricket on a track like this."

Cal shrugged. "Maybe this pitch is a bit more lively than the ones we're used to at the Priory but it'll get easier, you'll see."

"We won't have any batting left by then," said Marty, as Mack lobbed back an easy caught-and-bowled to a good slower ball from Alex Forsyth.

"Good luck, Hooker," said Azzie. "I'll come in next if you like – I think my nose has stopped bleeding."

I set out slowly for the middle. Erica came out to meet me. "I'm trying to get well forward to everything," she said. "But it's not easy when one ball's lifting off a length and the next shoots along under your boots."

"Let's try and see these two off and then attack the change bowlers," I suggested without much conviction.

Close up the wicket was even worse than it had appeared from the boundary. My first ball was quick and I played forward; it reared and pinned the fingers of my bottom hand against the bat handle. The ball dropped just short of second slip and I peeled off the glove to inspect the damage. My middle and third fingers were red and sore but I could still bend them – nothing was broken. I prepared for the next delivery. It was short of a length and thudded into my ribs. I walked away to square-leg, trying to keep my concentration. It was the end of the over and I noticed the scoreboard read 14 for three.

Erica played at and missed the next three balls which screamed through outside her off-stump. The next she played off her pads for a single and I was on strike again. The bowler pitched one short and I stepped back to pull it, which wasn't very wise on this pitch. It hardly rose off the ground. I tried to drop my bat on it at the last minute but it was too late – I was already through with the shot and I was square in front of the stumps when the ball hit me halfway up my pad. If ever there was a plumb lbw that was it. I scarcely needed a glance at the umpire to know that his finger was up. I was out for a duck without once laying bat on ball. So much for dreams.

As I passed Azzie returning to the battle he said, "Worse than Russian roulette out there, isn't it, Hook? Wish me luck."

I mumbled a couple of words of encouragement and walked on. Even Frankie, who was next in, was looking pensive and he didn't say a word about my dismissal. I sat down next to him and started to remove my pads.

"Bad luck, Hooker," he said finally. "At least you escaped with your life."

"It wasn't a good toss to lose," I said. "I wouldn't want to face Marty out there, would you?"

"Wait till he gets at them," said Frankie, with some relish.

"But we'll need a score for him to bowl at."

"I reckon we can blast them out for 30," said Frankie.

"We might have to," I said as I watched Erica ducking under another ball which rose from a good length and nearly took her head off.

At last Azzie received an over-pitched delivery from Alex Forsyth and he punched it over the covers for four. Maybe Azzie could work some of his magic in spite of the conditions. We were joined by Kiddo and Gatting who were both looking serious.

"I thought this wicket might be a bit lively after the rain," said Kiddo. "but I never expected it would have this much spite in it. If I were umpiring I'd be thinking about bringing them off before someone got hurt."

"Perhaps Bunter's playing a practical joke on us," said Frankie.

"Bunter's got nothing to do with it," said Kiddo. "He's done his best, but you can't prepare a good wicket from scratch in a few days. We might have got away with it if the rain hadn't come."

"So what are we going to do?" I asked. "How many weeks will it take to prepare a good track?"

"Who can tell? What Bunter would like to do is dig up one of the pitches and reseed it. But we can't play on one track all season. The best thing would be to lay an all-weather pitch alongside these two. You know – one of those matting strips. But it would cost a fortune and we can't afford it."

"How much?" asked Frankie.

"Seven or eight hundred pounds. Maybe more. Why?"

"Oh nothing . . . just an idea," Frankie said mysteriously.

"You can tell us about it later, Frankie," I said. "You're in."

"What happened?" asked Frankie, turning to see Erica walking back to us.

"Another lbw," I said. "Don't let it hit your pads."

As expected Frankie followed the same theory as Mack – there was little point in asking him to do anything else. Frankie is a natural hitter or a slogger, depending on the way you look at it. He has got a good eye and a strong pair of shoulders but his shot selection goes from poor to terrible.

Croyland opted for a double change of bowlers. They brought on their off-spinner at the Hereward Road end and another seamer at the other. Azzie watched the spinner carefully. He got plenty of turn from the track and the uneven bounce made him a real handful. Frankie didn't treat the medium pacer with quite the same respect. He pinged his first ball back over his head for four, swung wildly at the next and missed, and took the third hard in the middle of his chest as it spat off the pitch. They ran a leg-bye. Azzie was then given out caught behind, following a ball down the leg side which appeared to hit his shoulder rather than the bat. Tylan went first ball to yet another shooter.

29 for seven. We were now in the deepest trouble – particularly with Frankie facing the spinner. It was guile versus brute force and the smart money wasn't on Frankie. He darted down the wicket and swung mightily with his head in the air. The keeper had time to have his breakfast and lunch and then stump him but somehow he fumbled the ball and Frankie turned and fell back across his crease with a mighty thud.

"Timber!" shouted Tylan.

He hit the next ball straight up in the air. The bowler and mid-on collided as they went for the catch and the ball fell between them. After his two escapes, Frankie hadn't learnt a thing; he swung even more wildly at the third ball and this time he middled it. It came off his bat like a rocket, bounced once in front of us and flew centimetres over Gatting's head into the side of the changing hut. There was a splintering of wood and a crash from inside. Seconds later Ohbert came rushing out of the hut looking as if he'd had a bomb dropped on him.

"Oh but – it's exploded!" he cried.

"It's gone straight through," said Erica.

"Trust Frankie," sighed Tylan as he went to retrieve the ball. "He said that hut could do with a bit of ventilation!"

Frankie played all round the next three from the off-spinner, smacking his bat on his pad each time he missed. Then Jacky somehow managed to play out a maiden at the other end.

"I said it would get easier," said Cal. "If only our last four could put on another 20, we might have something to bowl at."

I feared that he was tempting fate and, sure enough, another double disaster followed. Jacky was run out by Frankie's call for a second impossible run and Marty went first ball, bowled between bat and pad. That was the fourth duck of the innings. And, in all likelihood, the fifth was on his way to the wicket. Ohbert approached the crease looking every inch the worst number 11 bat that Croyland would see all season. He looked up at the umpire and appeared to remember something. "Oh but . . . er . . . the middle one, please," he said and then forgot all about holding his bat up in front of the stumps and strolled off in the direction of square-leg.

"Play," called the bemused umpire and the spinner ran in for the final ball of his over. A late swish and Ohbert connected with the back of his bat and somehow directed the ball down to third-man; they ran two.

Frankie's next shot was his best. A straight drive over the bowler's head for four. Another four came from a top edge over the keeper and, going for the third boundary, he finally got the grubber which cannoned into the bottom of his middle stump. With another theatrical slap of his bat against his pad he walked off. Halfway back to the boundary he turned to speak to Ohbert and saw him still standing alone by the stumps at the bowler's end, unaware that the innings had ended. "Ohbert," shouted Frankie. "Time for tea."

We'd been bowled out in twelve and a half overs and we'd scored just 45.

HOME TEAM	GLORY GARDENS	V	CROYLAND CRUSADERS	AWAY TEAM	AT GLORY GARDENS DATE APRIL 26TH.

INNINGS OF GLORY GARDENS .... TOSS WON BY C.C. WEATHER FINE..

	BATSMAN	RUNS SCORED	HOW OUT	BOWLER	SCORE
1	M. ROSE	》	ct ARMSTRONG	DUFFIELD	0
2	C. SEBASTIEN	2·》	bowled	FORSYTH	2
3	A. NAZAR	4·1·2》	ct ARMSTRONG	BLACK	7
4	E. DAVIES	1·1·1》	lbw	DUFFIELD	3
5	T. McCURDY	4·2》	c x b	FORSYTH	6
6	H. KNIGHT	3》	lbw	DUFFIELD	3
7	F. ALLEN	4·4·1·4·4》	bowled	BLACK	17
8	T. VELLACOTT	》	bowled	BLACK	0
9	J. GUNN	1》	run	Out	1
10	M. LEAR	》	bowled	NOTTING	0
11	P. BENNETT	2	not	out	2

FALL OF WICKETS

	1	2	3	4	5	6	7	8	9	10
SCORE	0	6	14	15	22	29	29	35	35	45
BAT NO	1	2	5	6	4	3	8	9	10	7

BYES	I	
L.BYES	I·I	
WIDES	4	
NO BALLS		

TOTAL EXTRAS	7
TOTAL FOR WKTS	45 ALL OUT

SCORE AT A GLANCE

BOWLING ANALYSIS ⊙ NO BALL + WIDE

	BOWLER	1	2	3	4	5	6	7	8	9	10	11	12	13	OVS	MDS	RUNS	WKT
1	F. DUFFIELD	W	4	W	W	X									4	1	8	3
2	A. FORSYTH	2	W	4	X										3	0	12	2
3	S. NOTTING	2	4	W											3	0	10	1
4	J. BLACK	WW	M	#											2·3	1	12	3
5																		
6																		
7																		
8																		
9																		

Chapter Three

The pitch had eased a lot by the time Croyland opened their innings. There was still some uneven bounce, particularly at the top end, but none of the extravagant sideways, jagging movement there'd been early in the evening. Marty got a couple to lift in his first over but they weren't on target and the opener was able to leave them alone outside the off-stump. One went for a bye because Frankie let it slide through his gloves and then through his legs.

Azzie at first slip was a captive audience for Frankie's running commentary on the game. Fortunately Frankie isn't top scorer very often, but we all suffer when he is.

"You have to learn to play the ball late on a pitch like this, Az," explained Frankie. "You don't want to commit yourself to the shot too early, right? Just let it come on to the bat and *wham*!"

"I'll try and remember that," Azzie said tolerantly.

The Croyland opener played and missed. "See what I mean," said Frankie. "Me, I'd have been down the pitch to that one. It's a front-foot wicket, this."

Azzie nodded. "Front foot, head in the air, eyes closed. That's it, isn't it, maestro?"

"And how many did you score?" demanded Frankie. "Just seven, wasn't it?" Azzie smiled patiently.

The first four overs of pace failed to produce the breakthrough we needed and there were already 13 runs on the board. So I decided to try something different and brought Tylan into the attack. Ty turns the ball a lot and he can even bowl a top-spinner which races off the pitch. His regular leg break gets better and better because he practises it such a lot. "One day," he said to me at nets once, "I'm going to bowl a ball even better than the one Shane Warne bowled to Mike Gatting and people will never stop talking about it."

Tylan's leg break is spun hard with a sharp, anticlockwise flick of the wrist. Try and keep the side-on position as long as you can and don't let your left shoulder drop too early at the point of delivery.

Tylan's first ball was short and Alex Forsyth watched it carefully on to his bat; the second was a full toss which he dispatched with a flourish over mid-wicket for four. The next delivery was the top-spinner. The Croyland captain played for the turn and it went straight through him and clipped the off-stump. He looked back in surprise and then nodded at Tylan as if to say, Well bowled, mate, and walked off.

The new batsman didn't stay long; he fenced at a good length leg break – his very first ball from Tylan – and got the faintest of edges. Frankie appealed, fumbled, caught it again with one hand and gave Tylan a huge grin. "Howzat!" he roared. "Now for the hat trick, Ty."

It wasn't to be. However, Jacky followed up Tylan's successes with a wicket maiden and Croyland were 21 for three. All of a sudden, in the course of two overs, we were back in the game.

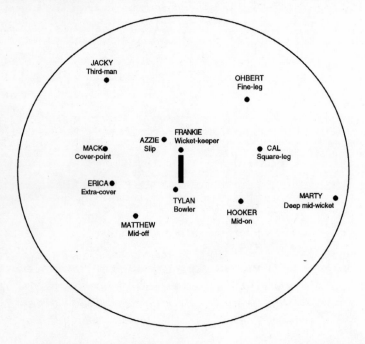

We still needed wickets, however – and that meant keeping an attacking field, even for the spinner. I had a slip and all the other fielders in on the single except for Marty who was out on the mid-wicket boundary. The new batsman rode his luck and started to hit over the close field. Tylan's second over went for eight runs and I decided to rest him and bring back Marty.

With the second ball of his new spell Marty got one to lift and move away. The snick took it to Frankie's right and he dived and took a marvellous one-handed catch only centimetres from the deck. "Hey, it's a pity we don't have action replays," said Frankie, getting to his feet. "Everyone should have a chance to see a catch like that. Straight out of the textbook."

"Almost as flawless as your batting, Frankie," said Azzie with a weary smile.

"It's the extra bounce in the wicket that helps him," said Cal. "I thought you were going to keep bouncing all the way to the boundary, fatman. Boing . . . boing . . . boing!"

The new bat took guard and faced up to Marty who came in off his long run. He came half forward to a very quick ball which pitched just outside off-stump. As his head went down the ball stood up and cut viciously into him. It struck him just under the helmet as he tried to pull away from it. He fell backwards and lay there without a sign of movement. Azzie was first to his side, and then Frankie.

"Don't touch him," shouted the square-leg umpire, rushing towards the fallen batsman. He still hadn't moved and no one seemed to know what to do. At last, after what seemed like forever, the batsman rolled over and groaned.

"Are you all right, mate?" asked Marty. The injured batsman didn't speak but he nodded. He took off his helmet and tried to stand up but his legs gave way under him and he fell back again.

"Don't try and move," said Cal. "Just rest a minute and get your breath back."

By now Kiddo had arrived on the scene.

"It wasn't even short," stammered Marty. "Definitely not what you'd call a bouncer or anything."

"Don't worry, son," said the square-leg umpire, "I saw it. It wasn't your fault at all. It pitched just here." He pointed to the spot. "Look, you can see where it's gone through the top."

Sure enough, there was a brown mark where the ball had dug into the wicket about two metres down the pitch from the batting crease. The batsman had now got to his feet again and, very slowly, he was helped off with a couple of his colleagues carrying his helmet, bat and gloves.

I threw the ball to Marty again. "Put that out of your mind," I said. But how could he? As he began his run he glanced over towards the pavilion and then sprayed a ball down the leg side. The next two balls were well wide of the stumps, too, and that made Marty more and more tense and angry with himself. Before long his rhythm had gone completely.

I came on to bowl at Jacky's end, but my direction was hardly any better than Marty's. I strayed down the leg side with my first three deliveries. Then I overcompensated and bowled short and wide of the off-stump and it was only a spectacular diving stop from Mack which prevented another four going on to their total.

I tried hard to relax and find some rhythm and after marking out my run up again, I pinged down a straight one which the batsman leant into. The ball must have stopped slightly on him because it looped back down the pitch, straight towards me, and I dived forward and took the catch. 35 for five.

Our only chance was to pick up another couple of quick wickets and I gambled on Marty's pace again. It was a mistake. His mind wasn't properly focused any more and I should have realised it. Although he tried hard, another wayward over cost us seven runs. Croyland were all but home. I managed to bowl a maiden and twice beat the bat but the inevitable winning hit came off Erica's fifth delivery.

Marty was first off the pitch. He rushed over to the gardener's shed to ask after the injured batsman. He was sitting up and talking and looked fine, if a bit pale. Their manager said they were taking him to hospital as a precautionary measure. Marty asked them to ring him and let him know how they got on.

The sliding stop and pick-up requires loads of practice. Mack begins his slide as he approaches the ball, his left leg bent at the knee. As he picks it up with his right hand he pushes against the ground with his right foot. His momentum brings him to his feet and he is now ready to throw.

"We didn't score enough runs," said Cal, as the team post mortem on the defeat got underway. "60 would have been a tough total to chase on that track but 45 was never enough."

"They had the best of the wicket too," said Azzie. "The first hour was evil."

"Tell that to the guy who's in hospital," Marty said glumly.

Frankie put an arm round him. "Come on, Mart. It could have happened to anyone. You can't blame yourself."

"I know that." Marty shook his head sadly. "I'm not to blame – the pitch is. And I'm not bowling on that track again. Not ever."

HOME TEAM GLORY GARDENS V CROYLAND CRUSADERS AWAY TEAM		AT GLORY GARDENS DATE APRIL 26TH

INNINGS OF CROYLAND CRUSADERS.... | TOSS WON BY C.C... | WEATHER F.I.N.E.

BATSMAN	RUNS SCORED	HOW OUT	BOWLER	SCORE
1 C. MARRIOTT	3·2 >>	ct NAZAR	GUNN	5
2 A. FORSYTH	2·1·4·2·1·4 >>	bowled	VELLACOTT	14
3 M. DEENOO	>>	ct ALLEN	VELLACOTT	0
4 N. ARMSTRONG	3·2·2·1 >>	c×b	KNIGHT	8
5 F. DUFFIELD	1 >>	ct ALLEN	LEAR	1
6 D. FRIAR		retired	hurt	0
7 S. BALDWIN	4·1·2·2·1·2·1	not	out	13
8 C. TODIWALLA	1·1·	not	out	2
9				
10				
11				

FALL OF WICKETS											BYES	1·1		TOTAL EXTRAS	3
SCORE	19	19	21	29	35						LBYES		TOTAL FOR	46
	1	2	3	4	5	6	7	8	9	10	WIDES	1		
BAT NO	2	3	1	5	4						NO BALLS		WKTS	5

SCORE AT A GLANCE

BOWLER	BOWLING ANALYSIS ⊙ NO BALL + WIDE													OVS	MDS	RUNS	WKT
	1	2	3	4	5	6	7	8	9	10	11	12	13				
1 M. LEAR														4	0	17	1
2 J. GUNN														4	0	11	1
3 T. VELLACOTT														2	0	12	2
4 H. KNIGHT														2	1	2	1
5 E. DAVIES														0·5	0	4	0
6																	
7																	
8																	
9																	

Chapter Four

Some people sleep on their problems and they don't seem quite so bad the next day. But Marty isn't like that; Marty's a worrier. Even though the news about the injured Croyland player was good – he was none the worse for his bang on the head – Marty couldn't put the incident out of his mind. He was in a black mood the following morning at school.

"I could have killed him," he said angrily after Frankie had made a well-meaning attempt to cheer him up by calling him Mad Marty, the 90-mile-an-hour Menace. "I may be a fast bowler but I'm not interested in knocking people's heads off. That track's unsafe and we shouldn't be playing there."

"Croyland didn't complain about it," said Tylan.

"Probably because they beat us," said Frankie. "It's amazing how winning stops you thinking about complaining."

"It needs more watering and rolling," said Jacky. "It's those big cracks which are causing all the problems. When the ball hits the edge of one of them you've no idea whether it's going to hit your head or your foot."

"Kiddo says we should all be wearing helmets," said Cal.

"But that Croyland guy was wearing one, and it didn't do him much good," said Mack.

"All the Stoneyheath batters play in them now," said Azzie.

"That's okay for Stoneyheath, but not everyone can afford them," said Mack. "They cost at least £35. And I bet they don't make one big enough for Frankie's head."

"If you've got a good eye and a classy technique you don't need a helmet," Frankie said casually.

"And what about those bruises you showed me after your knock?" said Azzie

Frankie grinned. "It's not a helmet you need, Az, it's a nose guard. Like the Man in the Iron Mask." Azzie's nose had turned purple overnight and it was still very swollen.

"So it's okay for Brian Lara and Sachin Tendulkar to wear a helmet but Frankie Allen doesn't need to bother. Is that it?" snapped Matthew.

Matthew and Azzie are the only players in the team to have their own helmets. Azzie only uses his on very bouncy tracks, although it didn't help him much yesterday because he'd taken off the visor. Matthew is a regular helmet wearer these days – he got in the habit on the Barbados tour where the wickets were extra bouncy. I'd already decided to use one next time I batted at the rec.

"Maybe we should just warn opposition teams that the track's a bit lively," said Erica. "Then they won't be able to sue us."

"You can tell them what you like," said Marty. "I'm not going to bowl another ball on that ridiculous pitch – and that's my final word."

Of course, it wasn't. Marty's not one to miss the opportunity of a good moan. And before long everyone at school was talking about Glory Gardens' new terror pitch and there were wild stories circulating about two players in intensive care and Azzie's nose being broken in three places.

Marty wasn't alone in his protests about playing at Glory Gardens. Frankie said we'd never get the pitch to be half as good the Priory, which was one of the best tracks in the county. "We've got to all work together to beat Whitmart," he insisted. "If we do, I'll bet any of you a fiver that we'll be playing at the Priory again before the end of the season."

And then there was Clive. Clive didn't have Frankie's

optimism or Marty's pessimism. Azzie and I next saw him at the colts' trial on Saturday afternoon. Marty was picked to play too but he made a last minute excuse about not feeling well, though we thought it had more to do with Wednesday's incident. Clive scored a fluent 39 in the trial match and hit me for two successive cover drives for four, as if I needed reminding what a good bat he is. Clive's a moody sort of person and I wasn't sure whether he'd be sulking about not playing for us against Crusaders or gloating that we'd lost. But he said nothing at all until Azzie cornered him. "Are you playing for us this season? Or are you joining another club?" he asked Clive outright.

"If I have time it would be great to play the away games," Clive said coolly. "But I'm not playing on that pitch at the rec."

"Why not?"

"You need to ask? Look at your nose," said Clive with a faint smile. "It won't be the last time that someone gets hit on that track. And the next one could be really nasty."

"You're not scared, are you?" persisted Azzie.

Clive's face clouded over. "Me scared? No way. If anyone asks why I'm not available, you can tell them that I play county cricket not crazy cricket."

When Azzie told Jo she was furious. "That's just typical of Clive da Costa. He always behaves like a spoilt brat. When did he ever do anything for this club? He's only interested in his own precious batting form and if he thinks he's bigger than Glory Gardens he can clear off and play for the stupid county, or Wyckham Wanderers even. Good riddance."

"That's a bit unfair," said Azzie.

"Unfair?" Jo rounded on him.

"That's right," said Frankie. "Clive can't help being arrogant, can he? It's like Marty being miserable or Ohbert being Ohbert."

"Or you being barrel-shaped," said Cal.

"Exactly." Frankie patted his stomach fondly. "We're all just born the way we are. Although I've got to say Clive's a lot better than he used to be and I don't think we should be too keen to kick him out."

"He's got a point about the pitch too," said Azzie. "Playing on a track like that all the time can't do your batting technique a lot of good."

"I think it's improved mine," said Frankie, playing an imaginary big, lofted drive. "I shouldn't be surprised if I'm top of the averages this year."

"If you are we'll finish bottom of the league," said Jo. "I don't understand any of you. How can you stick up for Clive? Why didn't he come along last Saturday and tell us exactly how he feels. He can't be bothered, can he? That's not being a team player."

"It doesn't mean the team won't miss him though," said Cal. "And if Marty doesn't play we'll be seriously under strength for Old Courtiers next week."

He was right. I'd been thinking hard about the Old Courtiers game too. Along with Wyckham Wanderers, they are probably our toughest opposition in the League. They, too, have four players in the colts squad and their captain, Rick Mattis, is one of the star all-rounders in the county. He'd scored a classy 48 against us last year before I got him with one of the best catches ever – *and* it was off my own bowling. We certainly couldn't afford to lose to them if we were going to have the remotest chance of retaining the title.

We'd played only one League game, but how things had changed since that first net practice. If I'd scored some runs or taken a few wickets, I might have felt differently. But all I could think about were the problems: the pitch and Whitmart, Clive and Marty, and the pressures of captaining a losing side. Perhaps it was time for someone else to worry about it all. Had I been skipper for too long, I wondered? Was I getting stale?

But whatever the future held, I was still captain for the Old

Courtiers game and I had to think positively. At least, I told myself, it was an away game. To be playing on a decent track again would make a nice change. And there was no question – with or without Marty and Clive, we *had* to win.

Chapter Five

Old Courtiers' ground is one of the prettiest around. It has a duck pond at one end and on a nice evening there are plenty of people sitting about and watching the game. The pitch is a beauty too. I won the toss and, unlike the previous week, I was very happy to take the first knock.

There was one change in the team from last Wednesday – Kris had come in for Ohbert. Jo had suggested leaving Marty out because he'd made himself unavailable for home games. It was a tricky decision because, apart from anything else, Marty is vice captain and the third member of the selection committee with Jo and me. In the end I managed to persuade Jo to drop her proposal, without mentioning it to Marty.

Frankie arrived at Old Courtiers on Wednesday evening looking even more pleased with himself than usual. He waved a copy of the *Gazette* at us.

PRIORY PROTESTERS TAKE FIGHT TO MINISTER

The headline ran right across the page and most of the story was about Eastgate Priory's appeal to the Minister of Sport but Frankie got a quote at the end of the article:

> *Junior champions, Glory Gardens Cricket Club, are orchestrating their own protest. "We think Whitmart is out of order," said their spokesman, Francis Allen,*

"and we're asking shoppers to stay away until they change their mind about destroying the Priory. It's sport versus shopping."

"Spokesman?" said Jo. "Since when?"

Frankie ignored her. "We've got them on the run. Listen to this." He took a letter out of his pocket and opened it. "It's from Walter Whitman himself."

"Who's he?" I asked.

"Don't you know anything, Hooker? He's the fat cat who owns Whitmart, that's who. I wrote to him, see. And this is what he says in reply."

Dear Frankie Allen,

Thank you for sending me the photograph of yourself showing your bruises. I am sorry to hear of your ordeal while batting so brilliantly last week. I was a wicket-keeper/batsman, too, when I was young. I can understand how you feel about the loss of your ground.

The decision to build the new store on Priory Road was made by the directors of Whitmart plc and I am not in a position to change this. However, I would like to help your club to improve the playing conditions at the Glory Gardens recreation ground. You mention the proposal of putting down an all-weather pitch in your letter. Please send me details of your plans because I believe Whitmart may be able to contribute from our local sponsorship fund. Good luck with your cricket.

Yours sincerely,
W. Whitman

"You're making it up," said Cal.

"I don't understand," said Tylan. "I thought Whitmart liked digging up pitches, not laying new ones."

"It's a bribe, of course," said Frankie. "To keep us quiet. But it's okay by me if they'll cough up for a plastic pitch for us. Let's get as much out of them as we can and still keep the Priory, I say."

"I don't know where you get your morals from, Francis," said Jo. "No one else in our family behaves like you. You're disgraceful."

"Why?" asked Frankie, trying to look innocent. "It's people like Walter Whitman who are disgraceful – taking away people's cricket grounds. He's only pretending that he can't change the board's decision because he's crafty. He's worried about the bad publicity and he's trying to buy us off. You've got to fight dirty sometimes when you're dealing with people like him. Maybe I can get him to pay for a new pavilion too."

"What was that stuff about your bruises?" asked Cal. "They didn't look too bad to me."

"Well, okay, I might have used a purple crayon to make them show up a bit better on the photo," said Frankie, stripping off his shirt. "But they hurt all right. I've still got one here – look."

Kiddo put his head round the corner of the dressing room and told us that the umpires were out and they were waiting for the openers. I wished Cal and Matthew good luck and then gave Jo the full batting order. With Clive out it looked a bit fragile after the first five. I pushed Frankie down to eight and he protested noisily, but I told him that Lance Klusener usually bats at eight or nine and he calmed down and went off to watch the start of the game, happily practising giant swings in the direction of the duck pond. I had Erica down at four and myself at five.

Two runs came off the first four overs and Cal faced just two balls and scored a single; the other run was a leg-bye. It looked like we were in for one of those tedious Matthew Rose innings which we knew all too well, but as he got more of the strike Cal started to chance his arm at the other

40

end and, after a couple of neat leg glances, he hit a glorious cover drive which dissected the field and raced over the boundary. Then Rick Mattis bowled two yorkers in a row, followed by a slower ball which Cal clipped in the air to mid-wicket for an easy catch. Azzie got a loose first ball outside the off-stump, went for an extravagant shot which was neither a cut nor a drive, and nicked it onto his stumps.

"Sorry, Hooker," he said when he got back to the pavilion. "That was a dreadful shot."

"Quite right," said Frankie. "You ought to be ashamed of yourself. Any decent batsman would have carted that into the duck pond."

Matthew at last got off the mark in the seventh over, but then he edged an away-cutter from Mattis straight to the keeper. The whole fielding team went up in an orchestrated appeal, and as the umpire raised his finger there was an enormous cheer and everyone rushed over to congratulate the bowler.

"All right, I can see they might be pleased to see the back of old Matt prodding away," said Frankie. "But why are they all dancing around like lunatics?"

"It's his hat trick," said Jo. "He took two wickets from the last two balls of his previous over. 14 for three. Put it up on the board, please, Francis."

14 for three didn't make great reading as I walked out to the wicket. Had I been right to bat first with our weakened line up? There wasn't much batting to come after Erica and me.

I soon realised why Rick Mattis had taken three wickets. He was swinging the ball a long way – mostly into the right-hander but occasionally he'd get one to hold its line. I nearly snicked my third ball to the keeper and then finally got off the mark with a little nudge down to deep backward square. It was my first run of the new season and I can't tell you what a relief it was to score it.

The bowling at the other end was a lot more friendly and almost straight up and down. I worked a couple of twos through the covers and was beginning to feel much more relaxed – when I stretched for a wide one going away outside the off-stump and spooned a simple catch to cover point. I couldn't believe it – it was such an irresponsible shot to play at this stage in the game and Erica's look told me that she thought so too.

I walked silently past the rest of the team, ignoring Frankie's comment – something about competing with Azzie for the worst shot of the day – and slumped down on a bench in the changing room. I hadn't felt this bad about my batting for ages. I couldn't seem to time my shots at all – but timing usually comes when you play yourself in. I wasn't giving myself a chance to build an innings because I couldn't concentrate. Nothing felt right when I was out in the middle. I closed my eyes for a moment and thought about my last big innings. I'd scored 54 not out in Barbados against Griffiths Hall with the ball coming fast and true on to the bat and the sun shining. The beginning of the season in England with grey skies and slow pitches is a different world for batters. My thoughts were interrupted a few minutes later by Tylan coming in to put on his pads.

"Mack and Kris are back," he said, in a matter-of-fact way.

"What! Both of them out?"

"Yeah. Mack ran himself out and Kris got a good one from the leggie. Frankie's in. I don't suppose I'll have a lot of time to put my pads on, will I?"

I rushed outside to see Frankie taking a wild swing at a well-pitched-up ball and missing by a mile and a half. Erica immediately came down the pitch to remonstrate with him but the grin didn't disappear from Frankie's face.

"Wasting her energy and her breath," mumbled Cal, and I had to agree with him. However, for a time Frankie proved us both wrong. He and Erica pushed the ones and twos and only once in the next three overs did he launch into one of his haymakers. What's more, he connected and the ball sailed over the mid-off boundary straight into – you've guessed it – the duck pond. As it splashed down an enormous cheer went up from the Glory Gardens contingent, and Frankie saluted his magnificent six with a punch in air with one hand and his bat held high in the other.

At the other end Erica was working the ones and twos brilliantly. Her best shot was a delightful leg glance off the front foot which not many cricketers play these days. She timed the shot so well that it almost beat the fine-leg fielder to the boundary.

It is the last split-second flick of the wrist from the top hand as the ball meets the bat which gives this shot its timing. Notice the position of Erica's head right over the ball at the point of contact. The weight is on the front foot as in a forward defensive stroke.

Between them Erica and Frankie doubled the score before Frankie fell to a sharply turning leg break which he nicked to the keeper. He was even trying to play a defensive stroke at the time.

With five overs to bowl, Rick Mattis brought back his opening bowler, and his pace was too much for Tylan who had all three stumps rearranged by a straight yorker. Once again there was the depressing sight of four ducks in the scorebook. Marty got off the mark with a single, edged through the slip area, and then Erica played the shot of the day so far – a pull between mid-wicket and square-leg for four, followed by a single off the last ball to steal the bowling. When Marty went, caught-and-bowled in the seventeenth over, we were 57 for nine – nowhere near good enough, but it would have been a great deal worse without Erica.

Jacky joined her for the last wicket and she gave him a long pep talk before he took guard to make sure he was on her wavelength. Jacky had only one ball to face from the spinner and he kept it out. Erica took six off the penultimate over; she was batting as well as I'd ever seen and in total control. With a new bowler taking the twentieth over and the score now on 66, there was a good chance of posting a half-respectable total. Jacky swung wildly at the first two balls and missed them both. He swung a third time and the ball skewed off a thick edge and cleared mid-on. They ran three. Erica squeezed the fourth past extra cover for a couple more and then drove the next ball hard but straight back to the bowler, who made a good stop. The final delivery was short, and she stepped back and swung it to the square-leg boundary where the fielder made a spectacular diving stop, but couldn't prevent them from coming back for a second. The innings ended on 73, with Erica's contribution an unbeaten 36. Both teams gave her a generous hand as she walked off.

HOME TEAM OLD COURTIERS V GLORY GARDENS AWAY TEAM	AT OLD COURTIERS DATE MAY 3rd

INNINGS OF GLORY GARDENS   TOSS WON BY G.G   WEATHER CLOUDY

BATSMAN	RUNS SCORED	HOW OUT	BOWLER	SCORE
1 M. ROSE	2·1 》》	ct FESTER	MATTIS	3
2 C. SEBASTIEN	1·2·2·1·4 》》	ct CHOWDHURY	MATTIS	10
3 A. NAZAR	》》	bowled	MATTIS	0
4 E. DAVIES	1·1·2·1·1·1·2·1·1·2·4·1·2·2·1·2·1 2·2·2·2·2	not	out	36
5 H. KNIGHT	1·2·2 》》	ct AGNEW	BENNETTO	5
6 T. McCURDY	》》	run	out	0
7 R. JOHANSEN	》》	lbw	CHOWDHURY	0
8 F. ALLEN	1·1·2·6·1 》》	ct FESTER	CHOWDHURY	11
9 T. VELLACOTT	》》	bowled	AGNEW	0
10 M. LEAH	1 》》	c x b	MELLON	1
11 J. GUNN	3	not	out	3

FALL OF WICKETS

	1	2	3	4	5	6	7	8	9	10
SCORE	11	11	14	19	20	21	42	46	57	
BAT NO	2	3	1	5	6	7	8	9	10	

BYES	1·
L.BYES	1·1·
WIDES	
NO BALLS	

TOTAL EXTRAS	4
TOTAL FOR WKTS	73 9

SCORE AT A GLANCE

BOWLING ANALYSIS ⊙ NO BALL + WIDE

BOWLER	1	2	3	4	5	6	7	8	9	10	11	12	13	OVS	MDS	RUNS	WKT
1 D. AGNEW	M	M	·²²	X	w·i	X								4	2	11	1
2 R. MATTIS	M	!·i	⁴w·wi	X										4	1	6	3
3 J. BENNETTO	·¹²²	²·²²	·i·i	X										4	0	19	1
4 D. CHOWDHURY	·w·i	·i·²	·²·⁰w	·²·i	X									4	0	12	0
5 A. MELLON	·i·²	⁴²²· w²	·²											3	0	14	1
6 A. BURGESS	·²²·													1	0	7	0
7																	
8																	
9																	

Chapter Six

It was hard to recognise the Marty who bowled that evening as the same opening attack bowler who had led us to victory time and again. If my batting had gone downhill since the Barbados tour, his bowling had dropped out of the skies. His first over contained three wides and a no-ball. But it wasn't just his lack of control that bothered me – there was no rhythm, no pace, no aggression, and without those things a fast bowler is nothing. Frankie didn't help matters by informing him that he was bowling slower than Tylan and asking whether he'd like him to stand up to the stumps. After two overs, Marty grabbed his sweater from the umpire and disconsolately walked over to me.

"Take me off, Hooker, will you?" he pleaded.

"What's the problem?" I asked.

"You tell me. I can't bowl on that minefield of Jo's and now I can't bowl here on a decent track. It doesn't feel right as it leaves the hand – I can't explain it."

"Take a blow then," I said, trying to sound unconcerned. "I'll bring you back at the end of the innings."

They had 19 up from four overs, and after such an appalling start I knew that our only chance lay in containment. Although Jacky was bowling well, I thought I might need him at the death, particularly if Marty wasn't firing. So I went for a double change and brought on Cal and Erica. They are usually the meanest bowlers in the side, especially Erica, who has an amazing economy rate.

Cal's opening over was a maiden, spoilt only by Frankie letting a bye through his legs. Erica started well from the top end; as Mack said, she's always straight on the money. But the Old Courtiers' openers are an experienced pair. They knew they were well up with the run rate and the important thing was not to lose wickets. Cal was turning the ball a bit and I thought hard about bringing Tylan on as a more attacking option. But, as Cal and Erica throttled back the run rate, it was too tempting to leave things as they were. In his third over, Cal gave us the wicket we needed. He drew Rick Mattis down the pitch with a slower ball which he read and hit over the bowler's head for four. Then, instead of panicking and firing one in, Cal bowled an even slower delivery wide of the off-stump. Rick launched into another massive drive and thick-edged it in the air to Azzie at backward point, who took a tumbling catch to his right.

The dismissal of their most dangerous bat didn't appear to trouble Courtiers, however. They reached the halfway point of the innings on 39 for one and now needed to score at just 3.5 an over to win. We wanted wickets badly.

Wayne Dailson was the new batsman. I'd heard a bit about him from Mack, who had played with him for the youth club side. Wayne is a big-hitting left-hander and, after taking his time to get a good look at the bowling, he opened his account with a powerful pull to the boundary from a rare short ball from Erica. Even though Cal and Erica had conceded a mere 20 runs between them off eight overs, we were still looking down the barrel when I started my spell.

I began badly again, firing down the leg side, and I was dead lucky to get away with conceding only two runs from three misdirected deliveries. Then I bowled one across Wayne Dailson and he drove it brilliantly through the covers. The shot had four written all over it until Mack, at cover point, dived full length, caught the ball in his right hand, did a complete somersault, and threw as he landed on his feet. The ball fired in, bounced once in front of Frankie, and slammed into his gloves right above the stumps. Frankie looked down the pitch at Wayne, who was struggling hopelessly to get back, and flicked off the bails. With a howling appeal he held up the ball in the direction of the square-leg umpire. The decision was a formality with Wayne two yards out of his ground.

The 50 came up with the last ball of my over and I walked back to my fielding position quite forgetting that I needed to bring on a new bowler at the other end.

"Oi, Hooker! Want me to bowl?" shouted Frankie.

I looked around. I had three choices. Tylan, Kris or bring back Marty. I wanted to keep Jacky for the end.

"Tylan," I shouted. "Keep it tight."

But we all know that keeping it tight isn't Ty's speciality. He's an attacking leg-spinner who often bowls an unplayable ball per over – but he's just as likely to bowl a rank half-volley or a long hop. He did both with successive balls. The short ball stood up and was dispatched for four over square-leg. The next was the googly which Tylan has only just learnt to bowl. It was pitched on a perfect length and the batsman tried again to play off the back foot, and was trapped dead in front as it spun into his legs.

I looked at the scoreboard again – 55 for three – the run rate, I calculated, had dropped to just above three an over from six overs. I decided to bowl one more and then bring back Jacky at my end. I managed to keep the ball well-pitched-up, forcing them on to the front foot, and some tidy fielding from Mack, again, and Cal, kept the scoring down to three off the over. What now? Tylan again? Or Kris? I'd already ruled out the idea of risking Marty in his present mood. Even though Ty had taken a wicket I went for the medium pace of Kris, who is usually reliable under pressure. She didn't let me down; her first over produced only one scoring stroke – a two behind square on the leg side.

Tylan's googly is bowled out of the back of the hand. The action is just like his regular leg break but, because the wrist is twisted right back at the point that the ball leaves the hand, the fingers impart spin in the opposite direction. The batsman expects the ball to spin away from him and is surprised by the off-break turning into the right-hander.

Jacky came back and was hit for a three and a two, and just as it looked as if they were strolling it he produced a beautiful nip-backer to knock out the opener's off-stump. 65 for four. Eight needed; three overs remaining. It was getting unbelievably tense – and, when Kris produced an incredible maiden with only a single leg-bye going on to the total, we began to feel that we had just a glimmer of a chance. The fielding was electric, the pressure on the batsman notched up a degree with every ball. A thin edge off Jacky went for two;

another leg-bye and a single took them on to 70. Jacky walked over to me.

"I'm going to try the slower ball, Hook," he said. "Can I have a couple out on the mid-wicket boundary just in case he gets lucky?" I took Mack out of the covers and dropped him out to mid-wicket. Jacky ran in and bowled and the batsman swung. For a moment I didn't pick the ball up. Then I saw it high on the leg side and Mack and Kris were converging on it. "Mack!" I shouted and Kris stopped. Was it the right decision? Had Kris been closer? Mack was at full tilt when he dived forward and caught the ball two-handed, centimetres from the ground. Somehow he clung on to it as he hit the deck and rolled over. For the second time in the innings Mack's fielding had come to our rescue.

Now it was all down to Kris. Could she bowl another over as good as her first two? I set the field carefully. We certainly couldn't afford a boundary; they only needed four to win. But above all we had to cut off the singles. Suddenly I remembered something Jo had told me. Because they'd only lost five wickets against our nine – if the scores were level at the end, they'd win. It meant that three runs was enough to give them victory. I brought Tylan in off the third-man boundary to save the single but I left Marty out at long-leg with Azzie covering for the dab behind on the leg side.

Kris's first delivery went for a single down to third-man. The next was in the block hole and Frankie pounced on it and prevented the run. Her third ball was hit hard into the covers and the batsman set off immediately. The non-striker had backed up a long way and was through for the single as Mack picked up on the run. Left-handed, he shied at the stumps at the bowler's end and an unbelievable direct hit left the batsman well short of the crease. There was a gasp of amazement. Neither the victim nor any of his team-mates could believe it, although we would have been half surprised if Mack had missed. Mack grimaced and clenched his fists. "Come on," he urged. "We're going to win this."

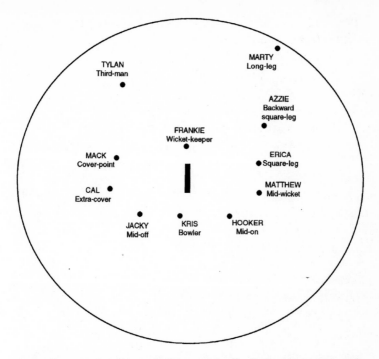

Another single came off the next ball, played between Erica and Matthew. It left the new batsman facing two balls to get the single they needed. He played at and missed the first, which fizzed by outside his off-stump, and for a heart-stopping moment it looked as if Frankie had fumbled and given them a bye – but he turned and recovered the ball just in time to produce a loud shout of "NO" from the non-striker. The batsmen conferred anxiously. Did they realise they only needed a single, I wondered? I brought the field in even closer and Kris bowled an attempted yorker on middle stump. The batsman swung, the ball looped in the air in the direction of square-leg. It was going over Erica's head. They had won. But no – at the last moment she shot out a hand as it passed over her shoulder. I looked towards the boundary and then looked back at Erica where she stood staring at the ball in her hand. Incredibly, she had caught it.

Frankie ran over and picked her up. And the rest of the team swarmed round to congratulate her. We had plucked an unlikely victory from the jaws of defeat.

HOME TEAM	OLD COURTIERS V GLORY GARDENS	AWAY TEAM		AT	OLD COURTIERS
				DATE	MAY 3rd

INNINGS OF OLD COURTIERS | **TOSS WON BY G.G.** | **WEATHER CLOUDY**

BATSMAN	RUNS SCORED	HOW OUT	BOWLER	SCORE
1 R. MATTIS	1·1·2·1·1·2·1·2·1·4	ct NAZAR	SEBASTIEN	16
2 A. BURGESS	1·3·1·2·1·2·2·1·1·1·1·1·2·2	bowled	GUNN	21
3 W. DAILSON	4·1·1	run	out	6
4 J. BENNETTO	1·4	lbw	VELLACOTT	5
5 D. CHOWDHURY	1·3·2·1·1·1	not	out	9
6 F. PIKE		ct McCURDY	GUNN	0
7 I. BULLOCK		run	out	0
8 D. AGNEW		ct DAVIES	JOHANSEN	0
9				
10				
11				

FALL OF WICKETS

	1	2	3	4	5	6	7	8	9	10
SCORE	35	48	55	65	71	72	72			
BAT NO	1	3	4	2	6	7	8			

BYES	1·1·1
L.BYES	1·1·1·1·1
WIDES	1·1·1·2
NO BALLS	1

TOTAL EXTRAS	15
TOTAL FOR	72
WKTS	7

SCORE AT A GLANCE

BOWLING ANALYSIS ⊙ NO BALL + WIDE

BOWLER	1	2	3	4	5	6	7	8	9	10	11	12	13	OVS	MDS	RUNS	WKT
1 M. LEAR	·1·1·1 ⊙ 1·3·2	X												2	0	15	0
2 J. GUNN	2·1	·1	·1	3 w 2 2 w 1	X									4	0	12	2
3 C. SEBASTIEN	M	2·1	·4 w ·1	·1	X									4	1	8	1
4 E. DAVIES	·1	2·1	1·1	·1	·1·4									4	0	12	0
5 H. KNIGHT	·1·1	·1·1	X											2	0	6	0
6 T. VELLACOTT	·1 4 w	X												1	0	5	1
7 K. JOHANSEN	·1 2	M	·1 1 w											3	1	4	1
8																	
9																	

Chapter Seven

At last we had a new player.

Without Clive and Marty, the full Glory Gardens' squad was down to 12 – 11 if you don't count Ohbert – and that doesn't leave any room for injury or illness. Jacky introduced him at nets on Saturday. The strange thing is that he lives next door to Clive, though Clive has never mentioned him. His name is Bogdan Woof – Bogdan's a Russian name, I think; his mother is from Russia. I don't know where the Woof comes from – but everyone calls him Woofy. Woofy is close to two metres tall – taller than Cal even – and unbelievably skinny. He bowls left-arm fast-medium with a slightly awkward run up and an action which is all elbows and knees. The result is pretty effective and, though he's not as quick as Marty, he gets a lot of bounce because of his height. The only problem is that he hasn't got any stamina, and he was completely exhausted after bowling half a dozen balls in the nets. I reckoned he would be useful in spells of two overs at the most.

Woofy took no time at all to fit in at Glory Gardens. He's friendly and cheerful and keen to learn. At nets he listened carefully to Kiddo's team talk which was all about applying ourselves when batting. "You can't sit back and rely on the other to make the runs," he said. "Everyone's got to chip in, especially the tail-enders. I want you all, but especially seven to 11 in the batting order, to take your batting practice a lot more seriously and concentrate on playing each ball on its merit. That means not swishing away at everything. Understood, Frankie?"

"I don't think he knows he's talking to the team's second highest scorer," said Frankie to me in a voice loud enough for Kiddo to overhear.

The first ball Woofy bowled in the nets was a beaut. To Frankie's immense delight he knocked over all three of Cal's stumps with a quick yorker. "It swung late," said Cal, ruefully picking up the ball from the back of the net.

"It was your bat which swung late," said Frankie. "He completely beat you for pace." From that moment on he and Woofy were almost inseparable. Frankie told him all about the club and its triumphs and recent setbacks. Woofy even seemed to enjoy Frankie's jokes. And it wasn't long before he became the third member of the campaign to save the Priory ground. They made an unlikely trio of rebels: the well-rounded figure of Frankie, skinny Ohbert with his Walkman and back-to-front baseball cap and Woofy towering way above both of them.

But no one, not even Cal, was laughing at Frankie's campaign any more. The promises that Walter Whitman had made in his letter were really taking shape. Kiddo told us that the all-weather pitch would be laid shortly and there was talk of Whitmart paying half the cost of a new pavilion too.

"I don't get it," said Woofy. "First they say they're going to plough up your cricket ground; then they give you loads of money for your new one."

"He's an odd geezer, Walter Whitman," said Frankie. "He's rich and powerful, and ruthless, too – but I think he's got a bit of a soft spot when it comes to cricket. And the funny thing is that I don't think it was his decision to develop the Priory."

"But I thought he owned the company."

"He does. But I reckon he lets the other directors get on with running it these days."

"Have you met him?" asked Woofy.

"No. He never sees anyone – not even the people who work for him."

"He's a recluse?"

"Yeah. He sends us letters by motorbike messengers and they always wait for a reply."

"What does he ask you about?"

"He wants to know everything. The results of our games. How many runs did we get? Who was the top wicket taker?"

"Perhaps he's just trying to be friendly."

"Not him. He thinks his money will keep us quiet and we'll stop protesting about Whitmart digging up the Priory. He's just pretending to be on our side. But he's in for a big surprise."

"What are you going to do?" asked Woofy.

"Walter Whitman may have the power and the money," said Frankie aggressively. "But we've got our backs to the wall and we're going to fight. They've boarded up the Priory but they haven't started work yet. So we keep bombarding them with posters and letters until we think of some brilliant idea to stop them."

After nets Jo produced the latest League table. Unfortunately Wyckham Wanderers and Croyland had both won their games and had the full 20 points. The new team in the League, East Street Bazaar, also had a one hundred per cent record after an impressive win against Stoneyheath and hammering Arctics the week before. We were equal fourth with Old Courtiers.

	Played	Won	Lost	Points
Wyckham Wanderers	2	2	0	20
Croyland Crusaders	2	2	0	20
East Street Bazaar	2	2	0	20
Glory Gardens	2	1	1	10
Old Courtiers	2	1	1	10
Stoneyheath	2	0	2	0
Arctics	2	0	2	0
Brass Castle	2	0	2	0

The rest of the weekend was very boring. Cal was away with his dad and I had nothing to do except brood about the loss of Marty and Clive and the team's recent performances. I couldn't help blaming everything on the move to the rec, including my own depressing form with the bat. Clive was probably right – that pitch *was* ruining my batting technique. And even if he was wrong, how were we going to win the League without him and Marty in the side? The victory against Old Courtiers had been more than a touch lucky and my contribution as all-rounder and captain had been pretty marginal. Without Erica's batting and her final brilliant catch we'd have suffered another defeat. Something had to change and the idea of stepping down as captain seemed more and more attractive to me. It would give me time to concentrate on getting my batting and bowling up to standard for the county games too.

The thing finally came to a head on Monday morning at school. I was in the cloakroom when Tylan and Frankie arrived. They didn't see me because I was behind a row of coats and before I could say anything to them Frankie spoke. "I think all four of them are the same," he said. "They reckon they're too good for Glory Gardens and they've all lost interest since we left the Priory."

"How do you mean?" asked Tylan.

"Playing for the county seems to be more important to them these days than playing for us."

"You're right about Clive and maybe Marty," said Tylan. "But not Hooker and Az. I can't believe that they'd think like that."

"You can't blame them – good players don't want to play on bad pitches. But how many runs have Hooker and Azzie, our so-called star players, scored between them this season? Twelve. That's not even half as many as me – and I'm supposed to be a slogger. Why don't I get picked for the colts?"

"Because you're not as good as Sam Keeping or Charlie Gale behind the stumps."

Frankie grinned. "I know that, you idiot. But all the same, maybe it's time for some changes at Glory Gardens."

"Such as?"

"A new captain? Someone like Cal who's not thinking about playing for the county all the time."

They walked off still talking about me. I was stunned. How could Frankie believe, after all we'd been through, that I wouldn't give one hundred per cent for Glory Gardens? I was doing my best, so was Azzie. It was just that the runs weren't coming. My batting for the county had been just as bad. Kiddo kept telling me it would come back. "Batting is half technique and half confidence," he'd say. "And you're just a bit low on confidence right now."

Fortunately I was bowling reasonably well, even though I hadn't taken many wickets. But it wasn't my batting that was bothering me most. Frankie had touched a sore point. His comments reminded me that I'd made some basic mistakes in the Old Courtiers game which could easily have cost us the match. I probably shouldn't have given Marty a second over and I'd kept moving fielders to where the ball had been hit rather than setting a plan and sticking to it. After listening to that conversation my mind was made up. It was time for someone else to have a go at leading Glory Gardens.

I had a word with Cal about it later in the day and told him what Tylan and Frankie had said.

"You're a bit sensitive, aren't you, Hook?" he said with a broad smile. "I'd get worried if I was starting to taking notice of anything Frankie Allen said. And you'll probably score a hundred in the next game."

"Maybe, but not as captain. It's time for someone else to have a go."

"If it ain't broke, don't fix it – that's what Kiddo says. We won the last game didn't we?"

"But I've had enough."

"Fine. Then take a break."

"Would you take it on?"

58

Cal laughed. "No fear. I don't mind captaining now and again as a stand in, but I'm not cut out for it all the time. I wouldn't do it nearly as well as you – and I'd hate to hear Frankie reminding me of that all the time."

"Then who do you think should take over?"

"That's difficult. Marty's the vice captain – but he's too messed up with his bowling right now. Anyway he says he's not going to play on Wednesday. If you ask me, Erica's the top choice. But are you quite sure?"

"Yes. The Arctics game will be my last as captain. I'll talk to Erica after that."

But in the end it was Erica who led Glory Gardens against Arctics – because I got flu. I was feeling so terrible on Wednesday morning that I didn't even care when my mother said that there was no chance of me going to school or playing cricket that evening. I slept all day until nine in the evening, when Cal burst into my bedroom and woke me.

"We thrashed them," he announced as he crashed down on the edge of my bed.

"By how many?"

"Well . . . actually it was a bit close. Are you well enough to hear about it?"

"You're not going home until you describe every ball," I told him, suddenly feeling a lot better.

The Arctics innings had been a rout. There was a devastating opening spell of three wickets for three runs by Jacky Gunn. Then Kris and Woofy took two each and the home team was skittled out for 35.

"And you knocked them off in how many overs?" I asked.

"I'll tell you the whole story if you shut up," said Cal.

"How many did you score?"

"Three."

"Only three?"

"Yeah, and that was the top score till Jacky came in. Listen to this," he read from the scorebook: "*Rose bowled Cameron 0; Sebastien lbw bowled Dade 3; Nazar caught-and-*

bowled Cameron 2; McCurdy bowled Dervish 1; Allen bowled Cameron 0; Johansen run out 2; Vellacott run out 0. That was 12 for seven."

"WHAT!"

"Azzie got a leading edge, Kris was beaten by a brilliant throw and I got a dodgy lbw decision – the rest was just suicide. Even Matthew played a cross bat shot and Tylan's run out was madness – he called for a second and he didn't even get halfway."

"What about Erica?"

"She was on two when Jacky came in. They played out two overs without scoring and then Erica pulled a short ball for four. I don't know what got into Jacky after that, but it's the best I've ever seen him bat. He didn't hit a single ball in the air and he placed his shots brilliantly, picking off the singles to keep Erica on strike. They put on fifteen, the highest stand of the match, and then Jacky edged their spinner to the keeper. Woofy managed to hang around till Erica had pushed the score up to 32 and then he was clean bowled. Mind you he's not got much more of an idea about batting than Ohbert."

"That bad? So what happened when Ohbert came in?"

"Erica said afterwards she told him to close his eyes and have a swing. Her theory is that whatever you tell Ohbert he'll do the opposite. So he played three great defensive shots nowhere near the ball. Then Erica got a single off the first ball of the next over. It should have been two but Ohbert forgot to turn at the crease and carried on running past the keeper."

"And then?"

"Then the bowler tried to york Ohbert but he managed to hit the ball with the bottom of his bat – you know that prod he does like he's digging the garden – and he immediately started running. Erica screamed at him to go back as the close fielder came in and threw at the stumps, but Ohbert somehow got his bat down in time and the ball flicked the off-stump and went past the fielder backing up, for four."

"And we'd won."

"With five overs to spare."

"How many did Erica get?"

"She made 16. She's batting really well at the moment. It's a good thing someone is. She captained the side okay too, in case you're wondering, although I think she changed the bowlers round a bit too much. But if you bowl a side out for 35 you haven't done much wrong, have you?"

I agreed. "Sounds as if she had a brilliant game," I said thoughtfully.

"She'll make a good captain. But are you still determined to give it up?"

"Yes."

"Fine. You're the boss – at least you were." Cal shrugged and then he suddenly smiled. "I'd better tell you the bad news about Frankie before you hear it from him. He took three catches and a stumping. You can imagine what he's like – he hasn't stopped bragging about it for a moment, and he's conveniently forgotten that he dropped a sitter off my bowling, let seven byes through and got a duck.

"And you missed Ohbert's catch of the season too. He was at deep square-leg and their opener top-edged a short one. It was in the air so long that we all had time to groan and pray and put our heads in our hands. Frankie was offering odds of 200 to 1. There was no way that Ohbert was going to catch it. The ball almost went into orbit and Ohbert danced about and ran round in circles but somehow he got right underneath it. His hands were waving all over the place like a windmill, and for a moment it looked as if it was going to land on his head and then, at the last minute, he grabbed hold of the bottom of his pullover and pulled it out away from his body and the ball dropped into it and stuck. The batsman was dumbstruck. It was brilliant."

HOME TEAM... ARCTICS ...... V GLORY GARDENS ...TEAM   AWAY TEAM   AT ARCTICS......
DATE MAY 10th..

INNINGS OF ..ARCTICS...................   TOSS WON BY Arctics WEATHER GREY..

	BATSMAN	RUNS SCORED	HOW OUT	BOWLER	SCORE
1	S.GOPOLAN		bowled	GUNN	0
2	J.HODGE	1·1·2·2·1·1·2·1·1·2	ct BENNETT	GUNN	14
3	T.PITMAN	1	lbw	JOHANSEN	1
4	B.SLEIGHT		ct ALLEN	GUNN	0
5	M.BLUCK	1	bowled	GUNN	1
6	D.MORGAN	1·1	bowled	WOOF	2
7	R.CAMERON	2	ct ALLEN	WOOF	2
8	F.DADE	1	st ALLEN	VELLACOTT	1
9	W.DERVISH	2·1	lbw	SEBASTIEN	3
10	G.NOAKES	1	ct ALLEN	JOHANSEN	1
11	P.ST HILL		not	out	0

FALL OF WICKETS										BYES	1·1·1·1·2	TOTAL EXTRAS	10
	1	2	3	4	5	6	7	8	9	10	L BYES	1·2	TOTAL FOR	35
SCORE	0	4	4	6	13	22	25	28	31	35	WIDES			ALL OUT
BAT NO	1		3	4	5	6	7	8	9	10	2	NO BALLS	WKTS	

SCORE AT A GLANCE

BOWLER	1	2	3	4	5	6	7	8	9	10	11	12	13	OVS	MDS	RUNS	WKT
1 J.GUNN	:¦ w	¦ :w	X	2 w										3	0	5	4
2 K.JOHANSEN	¦ :	w 2 2 :	X	: ¦ w										3	0	7	2
3 B.WOOF	¦ :	¦ w 2 w	X											2	0	5	2
4 E.DAVIES	: 2	M	X											2	1	2	0
5 C.SEBASTIEN	¦ :	: w	X											2	0	3	1
6 T.VELLACOTT	w 2 ¦	X												1	0	3	1
7																	
8																	
9																	

BOWLING ANALYSIS ⊙ NO BALL + WIDE

HOME TEAM..ARCTICS.......... V GLORY GARDENS..AWAY TEAM	AT .ARCTIC.......... DATE .MAY.10 Hₐ

HOME TEAM..ARCTICS.......... V GLORY GARDENS..AWAY TEAM | AT .ARCTIC.......... DATE .MAY.10.Hₐ

INNINGS OF .GLORY. GARDENS... | TOSS WON BY Arches WEATHER GREY.

BATSMAN	RUNS SCORED	HOW OUT	BOWLER	SCORE
1 M. ROSE	≫	bowled	CAMERON	0
2 C. SEBASTIEN	1.2≫	lbw	DADE	3
3 A. NAZAR	2≫	c×b	CAMERON	2
4 E. DAVIES	1.1.4.1.2.1.1.1.2.1.1	not	out	16
5 T. McCURDY	1≫	bowled	DERVISH	1
6 F. ALLEN	≫	bowled	CAMERON	0
7 K. JOHANSEN	1.1≫	run	out	2
8 T. VELLACOTT	≫	run	out	0
9 J. GUNN	1.1.1.1.1.1≫	ct NOAKES	MORGAN	6
10 B. WOOF	1≫	bowled	GOPOLAN	1
11 P. BENNETT	4	not	out	4

FALL OF WICKETS

	1	2	3	4	5	6	7	8	9	10
SCORE	2	4	7	9	10	12	12	27	32	
BAT NO	1	2	3	5	6	7	8	9	10	

BYES	I
L.BYES	
WIDES	I
NO BALLS	

TOTAL EXTRAS	2
TOTAL	37
FOR WKTS	9

SCORE AT A GLANCE

BOWLING ANALYSIS ⊙ NO BALL + WIDE

BOWLER	1	2	3	4	5	6	7	8	9	10	11	12	13	OVS	MDS	RUNS	WKT
1 R. CAMERON						X								4	1	5	3
2 F. DADE			X											2	0	4	1
3 W. DERVISH				X										4	2	5	1
4 P. ST HILL				X										3	1	9	0
5 S. GOPOLAN														2	0	6	1
6 D. MORGAN														1.2	0	7	1
7																	
8																	
9																	

Chapter Eight

I decided to talk to Erica before announcing to the rest of the team that I was standing down. She seemed surprised and shocked. If Frankie and Tylan were talking about getting rid of me, it certainly didn't seem to have occurred to Erica.

"Are you crazy, Hooker?" she said. "Why?"

"I think it's probably time someone else had a go," I said.

"Nonsense. You're doing a great job. I know we've got a few problems right now, with the pitch and Clive and Marty, but we'll get over that. We always do."

I shook my head. "I just don't think I've got the full support of the team anymore."

"That's simply not true. Who do you mean? If you're worried about Marty, he'll come round. You know that."

"It's not Marty." I didn't want to tell Erica about Frankie and Tylan so I changed tack. "Look, the real reason is that I want to concentrate on my batting and bowling for a bit."

Erica thought for a while. "Tell you what," she said. "I'll take over for the next three games on three conditions."

"What?"

"First, the others have got to agree unanimously. Second, that you'll be vice captain. I'm going to need loads of advice."

"And the third?"

"The third condition is, if we're still in with a chance of winning the League when we play Wyckham Wanderers, you'll take back the job again . . . if I ask you to."

I wasn't sure about that, or why she insisted on it, but I agreed all the same. We both decided that the best way to get the others to go along with the plan was to tell Jo first.

Jo was every bit as surprised as Erica had been, but, when she saw that my mind was made up, she agreed to help with explaining it to the others. She talked to each of them one by one and, although there was a good deal of surprise and protest at my decision, in the end Erica got the unanimous support she wanted.

To my astonishment the first person to tell me how gutted he was by the news of my resignation was Frankie. I wondered for a moment whether all those things about me that he'd said to Tylan had been just another of his strange jokes – knowing Frankie, anything was possible. I mumbled something about it being time for a change but Frankie had already moved on to more pressing things on his mind.

"It's definitely going to be laid next week after our game against East Street Bazaar," he told me.

"What is?"

"The new pitch. Wednesday's the last time we'll have to play on the track from hell, although the all-weather strip will never be nearly as good as the Priory. We'll have the new pavilion up in three weeks too so there's no need to mend that hole I made in the shed. Eastgate Priory are paying a third and Whitmart will cough up the rest."

"Two thirds? I thought you said they were paying half . . ."

"The Three Musketeers drive a hard bargain," said Frankie, smiling.

"The Three Musketeers?"

"Woofy, Ohbert and me. Wally may think he's a tough negotiator but he's met his match this time."

"Wally?"

"Walter Whitman, ruler of the universe. He told us to call him Wally – and who are we to argue? He says we should bowl first against East Street Bazaar, by the way. He thinks we're better chasing a total."

"Wally . . . Walter Whitman said that?"

"Yes. I suppose I'd better tell Erica if she's going to be captain now."

"How often do you hear from him?"

"All the time. He e-mails us now – sometimes four or five times a day."

"But you haven't got a computer, have you?"

"We use Ohbert's dad's. Wally's set up a Glory Gardens' website, too. Ohbert's done most of the stuff on it . . . so it's a bit weird."

"Hold on. You're telling me that Glory Gardens has a website run by Ohbert?"

"Yeah . . . they say cricket's a funny game, but wait till you see this. You might think it's impossible to play a sport and understand absolutely nothing about it – but Ohbert's made a breakthrough on that one. His match report of the Arctics game could have been written by a Martian."

"What else is on it?" I asked.

"All sorts of rubbish. For instance I told Ohbert as a sort of joke that I was a better keeper than Alec Stewart so that's up there, too. I hope Alec doesn't check out the site."

"Does it mention me?"

"Of course it does, we're all in it. You're the best all-rounder in the world, according to Ohbert. And there's an hilarious section on your fielding plans – did you know that the captain always fields at point so that he can tell people where to go and Ohbert's favourite position is deep fine-leg because he likes signing autographs on the boundary?"

"What does Walter Whitman think of the website?"

"He likes it. He's getting keener and keener on cricket every day. I think he'd sort of forgotten how much he enjoyed it when he was younger, before he became rich and greedy. Mind you he hasn't said anything about the Eastgate Priory Appeal. I wrote that and it's really good. It has only been up for two days and we've already had three e-mails supporting the campaign and one of them is from New Zealand."

I didn't know what to think of Frankie's latest piece of news, but for the first time I was quite glad not to be captain of Glory Gardens any more. Erica and Jo could handle Ohbert and his website. I'd stick to batting practice.

Saturday morning brought yet another crisis. When we arrived for nets there was no gardener's shed. All that remained was a heap of grey ash and a few black and charred planks which were still smoking. Someone had burnt the whole thing down in the night.

"It's unbelievable," said Jo, in disgust, as we stood around surveying the sad remains.

"Outrageous," said Tylan.

Kiddo said the fire brigade put it out just after midnight. I'd heard the sirens but I never imagined that it was our pavilion going up in flames.

"It's lucky we didn't leave the kit in there," said Erica.

"All that work and then some brainless moron destroys it," fumed Jo.

"Brainless moron? It wasn't you, was it, Frankie?" Cal asked.

Frankie grinned. "I've got an alibi. I was watching a late night film and Dad came in and took my telly away. That's the third time I've watched *Return of the Living Dead* and I still don't know the ending."

"It's really disgusting. The zombie turns up just when—"

"I don't want to know, Woofy," Frankie said firmly. "And anyway the zombie who did this wasn't me. But at least he's saved us the job of pulling down the old shed before the new pavilion arrives."

Fortunately the vandals hadn't torched the nets and we were able to get on with our practice session. Kiddo produced three brand-new helmets and announced that we all had to wear them in every game from now on. "Don't blame me," he said. "It's an official English and Welsh Cricket Board rule.

Every junior batter must wear a helmet, and wicket-keepers, too, when they stand up to the stumps."

"What?" cried Frankie. "That's disgraceful. I can't keep wicket in one of those."

"You can't keep wicket without one either," said Mack, laughing.

"Very funny," sneered Frankie. "I'm serious though. I'm not wearing a helmet behind the stumps or when I'm batting."

"Then you'll have to get a letter from your parents," said Kiddo. "You can't play in the League without one unless you have special written permission. The new regulations state that you must wear helmets even when you're facing spin bowling. That's a bit excessive, I agree, but I'm not taking a chance with anyone getting another knock on the head on this track. So helmets it is. Okay?"

"Not for wicket-keepers though," said Frankie stubbornly. "When did you last see Alec Stewart wearing a helmet behind the stumps?"

"He sometimes does to spinners on a bouncy track," said Matthew. "He's not stupid, you know, like some."

"It's not just wicket-keepers," said Kiddo. "Before long slip fielders will have to wear them too. The important thing is to start practising in a helmet in the nets. They take a bit of getting used to."

But Frankie was adamant and he said he'd get a letter from his mother before the Wednesday evening game.

Kiddo worked us hard on the technique for playing spin bowling. We'd heard that East Street Bazaar, the new team in the League, had a couple of star spinners, a left-armer and a leggie, as well as a brilliant number three batsman. Kiddo said that picking the flight of the ball early and using your feet were the mark of a good player of spin. And he showed us how to play the sweep to attack a good-length ball and get on top of the bowling.

Azzie plays the sweep shot with his head well over the ball, playing it down with an angled bat. His balance allows him to strike the ball late or early and direct it away from the fielders. The secret is not to try and hit too hard and it is safer to sweep with the spin. So a right-hander will prefer to sweep an off-spinner rather than a leg-spinner. It's also more dangerous to sweep on a bouncy pitch because it increases the risk of getting a top edge.

By now everyone had accepted the appointment of Erica as captain although Mack and Jacky both said to me that they hoped it was only temporary. I didn't know whether Erica had told them about her condition that she was taking on the job for the next three games only. She automatically became a member of the selection committee along with Jo and me. Since Marty hadn't come to nets we didn't have a chance to ask him whether he minded standing down as vice captain. We picked the strongest side we could for the East Street Bazaar game: everyone in the squad except Ohbert. But on Monday more disaster struck. Azzie was sick and we learnt that he was very doubtful for Wednesday. So Ohbert came back into the reckoning. The team was strong on bowling, with eight possible bowlers, but one of the weakest batting sides we'd put out in two years:

Cal Sebastien	Frankie Allen
Matthew Rose	Tylan Vellacott
Erica Davies (capt.)	Jacky Gunn
Hooker Knight	Bogdan Woof
Mack McCurdy	Ohbert Bennett
Kris Johansen	

Chapter Nine

Even if the Glory Gardens pitch wasn't as dangerous as it had been in the Croyland game, it was still very grassy and would certainly take plenty of spin. Tylan and Cal would play an important part in the game but first I was anxious to see how the East Street Bazaar spinners would perform.

We were playing on the second strip today and batting first – Erica had lost the toss. As the game began, everyone was standing on the boundary, anxious too see how it would behave. Matthew took guard and the opening bowler raced up to the crease. He wasn't big but he was certainly quick and his opening salvo went straight through Matthew's defensive prod. However, the first three balls came through at regulation height.

"It looks as if Bunter's got the wicket behaving itself at last," said Mack. He spoke too soon. The fourth delivery reared steeply off a length and hammered into the handle of Matt's bat. He immediately threw the bat down and tore off his left glove. Cal, both the umpires and most of the fielding side gathered round to look at the damage, and after a long break Matthew tentatively pulled his glove on again and faced up to the bowling. He got one well-pitched-up, outside the off-stump and shaped to drive. He didn't middle the ball and it rolled gently out into the covers, but as he made contact he dropped his bat again as though he'd been stung by a bee. He had another word with the umpires and finally walked off the field.

"I think I've broken it," he said grimly as he slumped down on the bench. Kiddo took a good look at the swollen finger and hardly gave Matthew time to take his pads off before rushing him off to St Cuthbert's Hospital for an x-ray. As Erica made her way to the wicket I realised I was next in.

Somehow she and Cal managed to survive the next three overs of pace with the ball hopping about like a rabbit and occasionally keeping low, too. All the runs came off the edge of the bat and Cal survived a fierce appeal for a catch down the leg side. Cal always walks when he knows he's edged one, so it must have brushed his arm or shoulder, but that didn't stop the East Street players round the bat grumbling that he was out. In the end the square-leg umpire told their keeper to shut up and get on with the game.

Dilip Singh, East Street's captain, soon turned to his spin attack and I began to see for myself what all the fuss had been about. The leg-spinner was the smallest player on the pitch but he bowled very aggressively with lots of rip and, unlike most leggies, he hardly bowled a ball that wasn't on a length. The left-arm spinner also gave the ball a big tweak and he varied his pace cleverly too. His standard delivery would swing and dip into the right-hander and spin away. From the way Erica and Cal played him, they were finding it a real problem to read his flight and length.

The score was creeping along and Frankie was getting restless. He soon let Cal know about it. "Wake up, dopey," he shouted and yawned loudly. "Get down the wicket to him and ping it back over his head."

"Shut up, Francis," said Jo.

But Jo was too busy scoring to keep him under control and, without Kiddo to restrain him, Frankie's protests got louder and louder. "14 runs off seven overs. It's not a test match, mate. Look, there's acres of room over here."

Then Erica got a shooter from the leg-spinner and was given out lbw. With the only in-form bat in the team on her way back, I suddenly realised how much depended on me.

Cal wandered over to greet me. "Welcome to the torture chamber, Hook," he said. "Perhaps you can tell me which way the ball is going to turn – because I haven't got a clue."

"Guess," I said unhelpfully.

The first two balls I received turned sharply past my bat and I began to see what Cal meant. This was up with the best spin bowling I'd ever faced and I knew instinctively that the only way I was going to survive was to use my feet and go on the attack. The next ball was a slower one and I waited for it and swept hard against the spin down to fine-leg. We ran two. The following delivery was almost medium pace and I went down the wicket to it and drove into the covers for two more. Finally I leg-glanced the last ball of the over for a single.

"He's caught up with you in three balls, Cal," shouted Frankie. "Wakey, wakey."

"Watch out for the left-armer's drifter. It dips into you late," Cal told me as we met in the middle again.

"I'll attack where I can; you keep them out," I said. "And don't take any notice of Frankie."

"When have I ever done that?" replied Cal, smiling.

I danced down the track to the left-armer's first ball and I found myself hopelessly stranded. I just had time to stick my pad out and block the ball or I'd have been stumped by a mile. We squeezed just four runs out of the next two overs and at the halfway stage the innings was floundering on 23 for two. The only good news was that we still had plenty of wickets in hand and I consoled myself with the thought that things can change fast in cricket. Cal hit the left-hander high over mid-off for the first boundary of the innings and then lost his middle stump trying to repeat the shot.

Mack lasted three balls and didn't get his bat near any of them; the third clipped his off-bail. Kris suffered the worst sort of bad luck; she was run out backing up. I drove the leggie straight back down the pitch and it was going for four but the bowler got half a hand to it and touched it on to the stumps. It was a complete fluke.

Suddenly I found that I was batting with Frankie, who had arrived at the crease determined to show Cal how to play. His first shot was a wild swing and he missed completely. I winced as the ball just cleared middle stump and went through to the keeper.

"Good ball," said Frankie, grinning back down the pitch at the bowler, who wasn't too impressed with his generous compliment. Frankie tapped his bat in the crease and looked longingly over towards his favourite mid-wicket boundary. The last ball of the over was in the slot for his slog-sweep and he didn't miss. It sailed over mid-wicket and beat the fielder at deep square to the chase.

The slog-sweep is a one-day specialist shot of high risk because it is played with a cross bat. Frankie picks up a good-length ball on the leg stump and plants it between mid-wicket and square-leg. It's important to watch the ball all the way and not lift your head before you make contact.

Dilip Singh immediately countered by bringing back his pace attack, which probably suited Frankie.

"Don't worry, Hook. I'm seeing it like a football," said Frankie, when I told him to calm down a bit. I could see that this was one of his barmy days; nothing I said made any difference. I decided to try and farm the bowling and for an over the plan worked – I scored a couple of twos and a single off the last ball. But then Frankie charged through for a leg-bye off the first ball of the next over and he was immediately attacking the bowling again with his big haymaking swings. After two air shots he finally connected and the ball flew high in the air over the bowler's head. The bowler, mid-on and mid-off all converged on it and then, as if by command, all three stopped dead and watched the ball plummet from the sky and drop right in the middle of them all. The next Frankie swing took an edge down to third-man and we ran one.

Happy, red-faced and sweating, Frankie came up to me again at the end of the over. "We're doing all right," he said. "I'll just keep crashing it about, shall I?"

"May as well," I sighed. "We've got six overs left. But try to get some bat on it – we can't afford too many dot balls."

"Aye, aye, captain. I mean ex-captain." Frankie returned to the crease and took up his crouching position as the opening bowler raced in. The ball lifted horribly off a length and flew past his ear. Frankie swung round and watched the keeper grope for it and miss and we ran two byes. The next ball was a slower one and Frankie was through with his shot when the ball passed him and struck the leg stump.

"How did I miss that?" he said to himself in disgust.

"I don't know, mate, but you did," said the keeper. "By about that much." He held his arms wide apart.

Frankie trudged off, shaking his head. There was no doubt that he really was taking his batting average very seriously.

Tylan edged a couple of runs before nicking one behind. Jacky got a corker of a ball which caught the shoulder of his bat and looped in the air, and again it was taken by the keeper.

And in came Ohbert. For some unaccountable reason he had persuaded Erica to let him bat ahead of Woofy. He staggered out to the crease hidden under his black helmet, looking as if he'd just been fired out of a cannon. I tried to say something about tactics. Mostly I said, Leave the batting to me and Run when I shout. But I sensed that even those words failed to penetrate through his helmet to the dark recesses of Ohbert's mind. He had a glazed look in his eyes which nearly always means trouble. The first ball reared at Ohbert and hit him on the arm. He sat down with a thump and all the fielders rushed in to see if he was hurt. Ohbert hardly noticed them. He rubbed his arm, jumped up and leant on his bat again to face the next ball. The famous "ohfensive" shot met a short-pitched ball and it squirted off the shoulder of his bat and looped over the keeper's head. "Stay there," I screamed, to no avail. Ohbert trotted through for a single. It was the end of the over and Ohbert had kept the strike.

The scoreboard read 48 for seven with four overs to bowl. I set my target on something around 60 and told Ohbert to run like hell if he hit the ball. Somehow he knocked it behind square and I ran. But Ohbert didn't. He stood there admiring his shot as the ball rolled towards the fielder, who picked it up and saw that I was hopelessly stranded in the middle of the pitch screaming at Ohbert. He looked at me with wide-eyed surprise but stayed anchored behind his crease. In the end I was run out by the length of the pitch.

"Unlucky, Hooker," said Woofy as I passed him on the way to the wicket.

"Unlucky!" I hissed. "Ohbert's the one who'll be unlucky when I get my hands on him."

Ohbert tried to run Woofy out off the very next delivery by taking a single to a ball he missed completely. The keeper only had to roll the ball at the stumps for the run out, but he missed and another vital single went on the total.

"Come on, Woofy," shouted Frankie. "Give it some welly."

Woofy tried. He tried four times and on each occasion bat

and ball failed to get close to each other. It was as if Woofy needed a longer bat and it would have probably helped if he had had his eyes open too. The last ball of the over rapped him on the gloves and, with neither batsman knowing where the ball had gone, they ran another single to bring the 50 up.

The next was the nastiest lifter of the day. It would have flown over the head of all the other players in the team, but Woofy pulled away from it and it hit him on the forehead, under his visorless helmet.

"That'll leave a nice bump," Frankie said heartlessly. But Woofy's head must be made of something exceptionally hard. After shaking it a couple of times he was ready to resume the contest. At last a wild swing connected and the ball looped into a space out on the leg side. Ohbert did his best to run Woofy out by rushing back for a second but again a fumble in the field allowed them to get away with it. Not that it mattered much. The next ball was slower and straight. Woofy swung so hard at it that he swung himself off his feet. The ball cannoned into his pads and, as the fielders appealed for lbw, Woofy's bat followed through and crashed into the stumps, knocking the lot out of the ground.

"I don't believe it," said Cal, putting his head in his hands. "He's as hopeless as Ohbert."

"He'd make a handy lumberjack, though," said Frankie.

With no sign of Matthew returning from hospital, that was the end of the innings. Our total was an inadequate 52 for nine.

BATSMAN	RUNS SCORED	HOW OUT	BOWLER	SCORE
1 M.ROSE		retired	hurt	0
2 C.SEBASIEN	1.1.1.2.1.1.4	bowled	C.TIKKOO	11
3 E.DAVIES	1.2.1.1	lbw	GURSHARAN	5
4 H.KNIGHT	2.2.1.1.1.2.2.2.1	run	out	14
5 T.McCURDY		bowled	C.TIKKOO	0
6 K.JOHANSEN		run	out	0
7 F.ALLEN	4.2.1	bowled	RANDHIR	7
8 T.VELLACOTT	2.1	ct MENDES	DOCTOR	3
9 J.GUNN		ct MENDES	DOCTOR	0
10 P.BENNETT	1	not	out	1
11 B.WODF	1.2	hit wkt.	DANSAK	3

HOME TEAM GLORY GARDENS. V EAST STREET BAZ **AWAY TEAM**
AT GLORY GARDENS **DATE** MAY 17th.
INNINGS OF GLORY GARDENS **TOSS WON BY** E.S.B. **WEATHER** Sunny

FALL OF WICKETS

SCORE	14	27	27	29	44	47	47	48	52	
BAT NO	3	2	5	6	7	8	9	4	11	

BYES	2.1
LBYES	1.1.1.1.1
WIDES	
NO BALLS	

TOTAL EXTRAS	8
TOTAL FOR	52
WKTS	9

SCORE AT A GLANCE

BOWLING ANALYSIS ⊙ NO BALL + WIDE

BOWLER	1	2	3	4	5	6	7	8	9	10	11	12	13	OVS	MDS	RUNS	WKT
1 RANDHIR SINGH	M	: i	X	: 2 W²	X									4	1	10	1
2 D.DOCTOR	: i	: 2	X	: 2	W W	X								4	0	7	2
3 C.TIKKOO	: i	: 2	: i	: 4 W	X									4	0	10	2
4 GURSHARAN SINGH	: i	W² 1	: 1 2	: 2 4	X									4	0	14	1
5 DILIP SINGH	: i													1	0	1	0
6 M.DANSAK	2 W													0.3	0	2	1
7																	
8																	
9																	

Chapter Ten

Matthew returned before we went out to field. "It's broken all right," he announced glumly, showing us his bandaged middle finger. "Just under the knuckle – you can see it on the x-ray. They say I can't play for three whole weeks."

"Then we'll have to field with nine plus Ohbert," said Jacky. "It's not going to be easy to defend a total of 52."

"We can do it if we keep it really tight," said Erica. "I want all the seam bowlers to bowl an off-stump line. That way I can set a five:three field and keep the pressure on them to score on one side of the wicket."

She opened the attack with Jacky, who bowled an immaculate maiden. Then it was Woofy's turn. He immediately got some extra bounce out of the pitch and Frankie did well to latch on to a couple of steepling deliveries which would otherwise have gone for four byes. East Street got off the mark with an edged four which ran all the way to the boundary, and then Woofy produced a beauty. It cut in off the pitch, seemed to gather pace as it bounced, veered inside the opener's defensive prod and clipped the off-bail. Frankie must have been distracted by the deflection and the ball burst through his gloves and hit him smack in the centre of the forehead. "Aaaaarggh! Howzaaaat?" He fell over backwards, still appealing.

Woofy rushed up to him – at first with a look of concern and then, as he got closer, he burst into fits of laughter. Both

79

he and Frankie now had identical round, red marks on their foreheads with the shape of the seam of the ball clearly traced diagonally across them.

"Well bowled, Woofy," said Frankie with a chuckle. "That was a knockout ball."

Kiddo came out with a pack of ice but Frankie waved him away. "That's why I don't need a helmet," he said. "Because my head's harder than the ball."

Jacky continued the good work in the next over as the other opener spooned his slower ball to Kris at square-leg. Then a complete mix up between their captain Dil Singh and the new batsman led to an easy run out. They were 12 for three when Erica and I came on to replace Jacky and Woofy after four overs.

Erica gave me the same field with five on the off and three on the on side, but bowling left-arm over the wicket means you have to bowl across the right-hander and that doesn't allow much room for error.

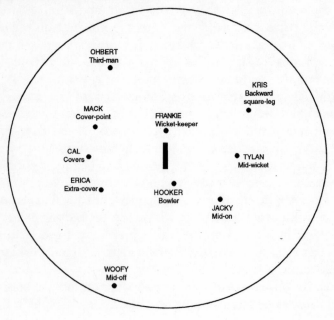

My second ball was a bit wide and Dil Singh lifted it with relish over extra-cover for four. Then I strayed down the leg, trying to compensate, and he flicked me for three more into the big empty space behind backward square-leg. I ended the over feeling pretty angry with myself and slouched off to my fielding position at square-leg. Erica followed me. "Do you want an extra fielder on the leg side?" she asked.

"No, leave it as it is and I'll try to bowl properly instead," I said.

Erica showed me the way with a lovely piece of accurate bowling which conceded just one run, and I found myself bowling at Dil Singh again. I dropped my pace for the first two deliveries and he played them both firmly into the covers. The third ball I gave everything and it flew past the edge of the bat into Frankie's gloves. Now for the in-cutter. I got it dead right – on exactly the right line and length, pitching on off-stump. The batsman was drawn forward into the shot and the ball cut into him and hammered into his pads. Frankie and I went up in a loud and confident appeal and, after a moment's hesitation, the umpire pointed his finger down the pitch at the East Street captain. I'd got him.

Two balls later I took another. The new bat inside-edged a rising delivery straight into his stumps. They were 22 for five and we were favourites to win for perhaps the first time in the match. Both batsmen at the crease were now left-handers and Erica had to rethink her fielding positions. She stuck with the off-stump line, however, and the fielding remained tight and lively with Mack in command and giving us the gee-up after every ball. The scoreboard edged forward in singles, byes and leg-byes and, at the halfway point, they were on 32.

I was annoyed when Erica took me off and replaced me with Tylan at the top end. Tylan prefers to bowl to right-handers and his first delivery was a full toss which was swung high in the air down to backward square-leg, where the lone figure of Ohbert stood thinking about everything except the ball heading fast in his direction at head height.

"Ohbert!" we all shouted, and he looked up – just in time to raise two hands vaguely in the direction of the approaching danger. *Smack!* It burst through his fingers and struck him a sickening crack on the forehead. Ohbert fell back like a skittle going down and the ball bounced away back towards the wicket again, where Kris rushed in to collect it. The stunned batsmen hesitated and managed only a single. The stunned Ohbert rose unsteadily to his feet and wobbled a bit.

"Oh but, sorry, I dropped it," he said.

"Oh but, Ohbert, you stopped it. That's the main thing," said Mack.

"And you've got the red mark on your forehead," said Frankie. "Welcome to the club, Ohbert. The Three Nutters." Ohbert felt the bump and beamed with pleasure. And he too waved away Kiddo and his ice pack.

Tylan bowled again and the batsman went for the sweep. From mid-on I saw the bail fall and I saw Frankie look at Old Sid, our umpire, first with a smile, then in amazement and then, after a second or two more, he appealed. "Not out," said Sid.

"Not out? It was clean bowled," blurted Frankie. The batsman shook his head. Erica picked up the ball and told Frankie to get on with the game. "But how could it be anything else but clean bowled. He was bowled round his legs," insisted Frankie.

"You know what happened," said the batsman, looking Frankie straight in the eye.

"Too right I do," said Frankie. "It hit your leg stump."

"And I saw you knock the bail off with your glove."

"What?"

"Shut up, Frankie," said Erica firmly, throwing the ball to Tylan.

Frankie let the next ball through his legs for a bye, and he rushed frantically after it and shied angrily at the stumps. Then Tylan was smacked over the top for four and suddenly Bazaar needed just 13 for victory. Erica had a brief word with

Tylan and he ran in and bowled his googly. The batter came forward, misread the spin and paddled it back off a leading edge for an easy caught-and-bowled.

Erica finished her spell with another maiden, with just one leg-bye coming off it, to give her the astonishing figures of 4 overs; 5 runs; 0 wickets.

Tylan's next over was a loose one and he would have conceded far more than five runs without some brilliant fielding by Erica and Mack. But now the target was just eight away and Erica turned to Jacky again. It was the last throw of the dice – and it worked. His second ball did the trick, getting the edge through to Frankie, and his fourth produced a convincing shout for lbw which Old Sid again turned down. He doesn't give many lbws unless you're on the back foot, plumb in front.

Bazaar still crept closer to their target with Frankie's least favourite left-hander calling all the shots. And yet again we pegged them back. Kris had the new bat caught at mid-off by Cal and, at the other end, Jacky responded with a corker of a delivery which ripped out the number ten's middle stump. Suddenly their last pair were at the wicket needing six for victory. Erica brought in the field and the new bat edged behind for a single.

The last ball of Jacky's over was a slower ball and the number five bat chanced his arm and hit over the top. It looked like a boundary all the way but Mack was off after it like an Australian rabbit – his sliding stop and throw kept the runs down to two and it also left the number 11 on strike for the start of Kris's next over.

That made it 50 for nine. The position was clear for all to see – we took the last wicket or we lost. Kris bowled a straight one at the number 11; he missed it and the ball just cleared middle stump. Frankie caught the ball and left the batsman in no doubt about how lucky he was to still be there. Kris bowled again and the ball looped up off bat and pad just short of Jacky at shortish square-leg. The next squirted between gully and cover point and the left-hander turned down an easy single. The pressure was getting to them too. But Kris kept her cool for the rest of the over and the score remained on 50.

Who would Erica turn to now? Jacky was bowled out and so was she. I had one over left and Woofy two. She surprised everyone by flicking the ball to Cal. Cal against the left-hander with three runs needed. The tension was mounting with every move, every field placing. Finally Cal was ready. He ran in and bowled. I could see from his action that he gave the ball a big tweak.

Cal bowls round the wicket to the left-hander. Notice how the left side of his body is braced at the point of delivery. The high arm action gives him the extra bounce. Here he bowls close to the stumps so that the flight is on the line of the off-stump.

The batsman went forward to him and the ball turned and lifted and took the glove. It looped in the air on the off-side and for a moment seemed to hang there. Frankie lurched forward and at the last second his left hand scooped under the ball and he held on. "Owzaaaaat!" The batsman turned and walked. "And that's the end of your second innings," said Frankie, triumphantly.

HOME TEAM	GLORY GARDENS V EAST STREET BAZ	AWAY TEAM	AT GLORY GARDENS DATE MAY 17th

INNINGS OF EAST STREET BAZAAR | TOSS WON BY E.S.B. | WEATHER Sunny

BATSMAN	RUNS SCORED	HOW OUT	BOWLER	SCORE
1 HARDEEP SINGH	1 >>	ct JOHANSEN	GUNN	1
2 A. BHINDY	4 >>	bowled	WOOF	4
3 DILIP SINGH	1·2·1·4·3·1 >>	lbw	KNIGHT	12
4 C. TIKKOO	>>	run	out	0
5 IAN SINGH	2·1·1·1·1·1·1·1·2 >>	ct ALLEN	SEBASTIEN	12
6 M. DANSAK	2 >>	bowled	KNIGHT	2
7 RANDIR SINGH	1·1·1·4 >>	c x b	VELLACOTT	7
8 D. DOCTOR	1·1 ·	ct ALLEN	GUNN	2
9 MOHINDER SINGH	1	ct SEBASTIEN	JOHANSEN	1
10 D. MENDES	>>	bowled	GUNN	0
11 GURSHARAN S.		not	out	0

FALL OF WICKETS											BYES	2·1	TOTAL EXTRAS	9
SCORE	4	8	12	20	22	30	45	47	47	50	L.BYES	·1·1·1	TOTAL FOR WKTS	50 ALL OUT
	1	2	3	4	5	6	7	8	9	10	WIDES			
BAT NO	2	1	4	3	6	7	8	9	10	5	NO BALLS	1		

BOWLER	BOWLING ANALYSIS ⊙ NO BALL + WIDE													OVS	MDS	RUNS	WKT
	1	2	3	4	5	6	7	8	9	10	11	12	13				
1 J. GUNN	M	⋮ẇ⋮	X	ẇ⋮	⋮ẇ₂	X								4	1	6	3
2 B. WOOF	⋮ẇ₂⋮ 4·6·	X												2	0	8	1
3 H. KNIGHT	4·3⋮ẇ₂⋮	i	X											3	0	12	2
4 E. DAVIES	⋮ ⋮2⋮ ⋮	M	X											4	1	5	0
5 T. VELLACOTT	! 4⋮ ⋮	X												2	0	10	1
6 K. JOHANSEN	⋮ẇ M													2	1	1	1
7 C. SEBASTIEN	ẇ													0·1	0	0	1
8																	
9																	

Chapter Eleven

Glory Gardens' victory celebrations were led by the Three Nutters with their identical red bumps smack in the middle of their foreheads.

"No one can ever say we don't get our heads behind the ball," said Woofy, as the three of them posed in front of Jo for a photo.

"Did anyone notice how the ball went out of shape after Frankie head-butted it?" said Cal.

Woofy did an impersonation of a red traffic light and Frankie drew a face on his bump so that it looked as if a little red-faced dwarf was peering out of his forehead. Even Ohbert appeared to see the joke. "Oh but can I have a copy of the picture to put up on the website?" he said to Jo. This was the first Jo had heard of the Glory Gardens' site and she quizzed Ohbert about it suspiciously.

"I've got an idea for a new page," said Frankie. "We'll call it 'Blind Pugh's Bloomers'."

"Who's Blind Pugh?" I asked.

"Old Sid, of course. That ball hit the stumps; anyone could see that. What was that stupid rubbish about me knocking off the bail? If Sid had given him out we'd have won easily."

"Are you sure you didn't just touch the wicket? That bang on the head might have confused you," Cal said mischievously.

Frankie took the bait. "Of course I didn't. I'm too skilful a wicket-keeper for that. He was clean bowled, wasn't he, Tylan?"

"I couldn't see properly," said Ty. "The batter was between me and the stumps."

"And they didn't seem to be a cheating sort of team to me," said Matthew, cagily.

Cal could see that Frankie was getting angry and he stepped in. "I'm glad he wasn't given out," he said. "If he'd gone we'd have missed that bouncy catch of yours at the end, fatman. It was the champagne moment."

"Yeah, I got him in the end," said Frankie with a broad smile of satisfaction.

Jo managed to collect together the rest of the evening's results before we left. It wasn't particularly good news. Wyckham had beaten Old Courtiers and gone top of the League with 40 points. Nothing upsets Glory Gardens more than being second to Wyckham Wanderers. Not that there's anything wrong with them as individuals – everyone likes Charlie Gale, their wicket-keeper, and Youz Mohamed and Win Reifer and, although Liam "Big Head" Katz, the Wanderers' skipper, can be even more arrogant than Clive, he's without a doubt one of the best all-rounders in the county. But we hate losing to Wyckham and they were the form team of the moment. We were down to play them in the seventh and final round of League fixtures. It was bound to be a crunch match but before that we had to beat Stoneyheath and Brass Castle.

	PLAYED	WON	LOST	POINTS
Wyckham Wanderers	4	4	0	40
Croyland Crusaders	4	3	1	30
East Street Bazaar	4	3	1	30
Glory Gardens	4	3	1	30
Old Courtiers	4	1	3	10
Stoneyheath	4	1	3	10
Arctics	4	1	3	10
Brass Castle	4	0	4	0

On Friday it started raining. It rained all day Saturday and nets were called off. It rained most of the week and all four League games were cancelled too. The laying of the new pitch at the rec had to be postponed. And worst of all, Jacky injured his ankle playing five-a-side football. He said he could bowl with his ankle strapped up but it looked badly swollen, and without Jacky we were down to ten players for the Brass Castle game. Nine if you don't count Ohbert.

Erica suggested asking Marty or Clive to play but Jo was dead set against it. "They've walked away from Glory Gardens. I'd rather play with ten than crawl to those two to come back." And, as usual, Jo got her way.

Defending our League title without Clive, Matthew, Marty, and possibly Jacky, was a daunting thought and, although Azzie was back, the team sheet Jo passed round on the Saturday morning before the Brass Castle game didn't make happy reading:

Cal Sebastien	Kris Johansen
Erica Davies	Tylan Vellacott
Azzie Nazar	Bogdan Woof
Hooker Knight	Jacky Gunn
Mack McCurdy	Ohbert Bennett
Frankie Allen	

"I'm going to open the batting with me and Cal," Erica told me. "We've only got four specialist batters, so at least one of us will have to be in the runs."

"If Jacky breaks down we'll be struggling for bowlers too," I said. "Woofy and I are the only quicks and he has to go and lie down after an over and a half."

"We'll manage," said Erica brightly. "What do you think of the new track?"

Four workmen were out in the middle putting the finishing touches to the all-weather pitch, and the rest of the Glory Gardens players were standing around watching with Kiddo and Gatting.

"It'll be a lot better to bat on than before," I said.

"But not as good as the Priory," said Erica, as if reading my mind. "Still, at least we won't be facing Win Reifer on a wicket where the ball's lifting round your ears."

Win is Wyckham Wanderers extra quick attack bowler and the prospect of him hammering the ball in short on one of the grass tracks at the rec wasn't a pleasant thought.

Kiddo finally called everyone together for the practice session and introduced us to another new fielding exercise.

Four fielders took part with Azzie and me on one side and Cal and Mack on the other. We jogged round a single stump in an anticlockwise direction and Kiddo rolled the ball for each of us in turn to pick up on the run and shy at the stump with our partner backing up the throw. You get five points for a direct hit on the stump and lose a point for a misfield.

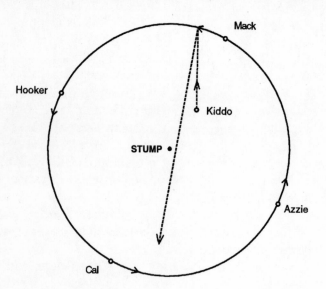

Kiddo rolls the ball ahead of Mack who picks up and shies at the single stump on the run

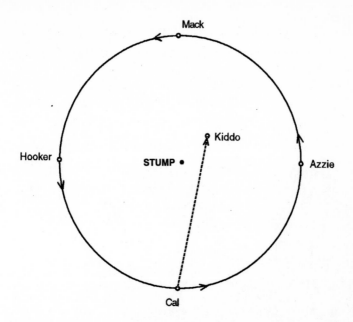

Cal backs up the throw and then returns the ball to Kiddo who now rolls it to Hooker... and so on.

Mack got four direct hits and Azzie one before Kiddo told us to jog round in the opposite direction, which meant you had to pick up with your left hand. That made it easier for me because I throw left-handed and I had two direct hits. So did Mack, who throws equally well with either hand. The session was hard work – jogging, sprinting, diving and throwing – and in the end Mack and Cal won by 36 points to 29. Mack threw the stump down with nearly half of his attempts and none of his throws missed by more than a few centimetres.

Later, in the nets, Kiddo gave me some help with getting forward or back to good-length fast bowling.

"You're getting caught on the crease too often," he said. "You've got to be more decisive about going on to the front foot or the back foot, and with a good length ball that will depend on the bounce and pace of the pitch. If the bounce is low you need to step out and meet the ball. If it's high, you're a good back-foot player, so play back and give yourself time.

If the pitch is slow and low the best approach is to play forward decisively to a good length ball. On a bouncy pitch it may be better to play more off the back foot. But whatever you do, don't get caught in two minds.

We had a practice bowl on the all-weather pitch before we left and Frankie told us that the new pavilion would also be ready before the Wyckham game. "Wally says we should have an opening ceremony. What do you think?"

"Will he come?" asked Erica.

"No chance. I told you he never goes anywhere; he's a hermit. But if we let on to him we're having a barbecue, I bet he'll send loads of food from Whitmart. I could order hamburgers and sausages and . . ."

"But we can't keep taking stuff from that man, Francis," said Jo.

"Why not? He took our cricket pitch away from us, didn't he? And whatever he thinks, he's going to give it back to us in the end. We'll make sure of that, you'll see."

"Are you up to something wicked, Frankie?" asked Cal.

"Me?" said Frankie with an innocent smile.

Chapter Twelve

Clive could have chosen a better time to turn up to the Brass Castle ground. The home side was batting and we were suffering badly in the field.

"What's the score?" he asked casually as he approached Jo and Jacky, who were sitting together on a bench by the pavilion.

"Oh, it's you," said Jo, fixing him with a chilling glare. "It's 61 for three, if you must know."

"Hooker's taken all the wickets," said Jacky.

"Why aren't you bowling?" asked Clive.

"I've done my ankle. It gave way again when I was warming up before the start of the game. Look." Jacky rolled up his left trouser leg and took off the ice pack which was wrapped round his ankle in a towel.

"Ugh! It looks like an orange is growing out of it," said Clive.

"What are you doing here?" Jo asked coldly, without looking up from her scorebook. "If you'd come earlier you could have played for us. We've only got ten out there now."

"Oh," said Clive. Then his face brightened and he stood up. "I've got my kit with me. Why shouldn't I play?"

"Because you're not really a Glory Gardens player, are you?" muttered Jo.

"Oh, you don't think so?"

"There hasn't been much sign of it this season."

Clive didn't reply and strode off towards the dressing room in the Brass Castle pavilion. Minutes later he emerged in his whites and stood on the boundary, waving at me.

"Hooker's not captain any more," yelled Jacky. "Erica's in charge."

"Erica!" said Clive, with a momentary look of disapproval.

At the end of the over Erica beckoned him on to the pitch. By the time he joined us Brass Castle were 70 for four with four and a half overs to bowl and Tylan had just taken a wicket.

"Cover-point, Clive," said Erica, as if he'd been on the pitch all evening.

Tylan's second over was a mixture of all-sorts. Kiddo tells him to bowl his leg break for five out of six balls and keep the googly or the top-spinner as a surprise ball. But Tylan likes to experiment all the time. He sprayed a quicker ball down the leg side for a wide and then dropped one short which was dispatched square on the off. The next ball was a beauty: bowled on leg stump, it straightened and, as the batsman went to flick it square, bowled him round his legs.

At the end of Ty's over Erica called me on again. I'd had a spell of two at the top end and one at the bottom end, and so far taken three for 15. This would be my last over – and if I've got one criticism of Erica as captain it's that she chops and changes the bowlers around too much so no one can settle into a rhythm. Al Rasteau, their opening bat, was facing and he was now on 39 and playing with great confidence. Twice I beat him with away swingers outside the off-stump; then he drove me into the covers for two. I walked back thinking, "in-dipping yorker". I gripped the ball with the seam running straight between my first two fingers and set my sights firmly on the off-stump. It felt really good as it left my hand. In the follow-through I saw Al go for the big drive again and there was an audible snick. Frankie was going the wrong way for the inside edge but he stuck out his left hand and the ball stuck. He beamed at me as he threw it up in triumph.

I persuaded Erica to give me two slips for the new batter, and two balls later I got the pay off when he snicked a swinging ball to Cal at second slip. It was a stunning catch.

Cal takes this difficult catch low to his right. He makes it look easy because he keeps still and in the crouching position as the ball takes the edge. Notice Azzie, too, at first slip with his eyes on the ball, ready to spring if Cal doesn't take it cleanly.

It was my fifth wicket – five for 17, my best figures ever. But, even though we had two new players at the crease, we failed to press home our advantage. Woofy dropped a sitter off Erica's next over which went for eight runs, wildly expensive by her standards. Then the Brass Castle umpire turned down two close lbw appeals from Kris. In the end they finished on 91 for seven. It was a big total but, on a firm, flat pitch, just about gettable.

Frankie thought so. "Without Matthew clogging things up, we should knock those off in ten overs," he said confidently. He even suggested to Erica that he should go in as an opening pinch hitter to get the innings off to a roaring start.

But Erica stuck to her plan and opened with Cal and herself. By the end of the first over they were both back in the pavilion – Erica played on and Cal was caught off a leading edge, the ball lobbing back to the bowler.

Azzie and I came together in the middle and I had a strange, confident feeling that we were going to put on a score together for the first time this season. Azzie was timing the ball sweetly and I hit a couple of cracking off-drives. In the space of six overs we had sped up to 40 and it began to look as if Frankie's prediction might be right. But again there was a double disaster. First Azzie pulled a short ball straight down square-leg's throat. The ball was travelling at a hundred miles an hour but he made the catch look easy. A couple of minutes later, I played too early at a slower ball and lifted a simple chance to mid-off.

Frankie soon made it five wickets down – a typical head in the air heave struck high on the bat, which gave mid-wicket an easy piece of catching practice. Suddenly the long Glory Gardens' tail was exposed with only Clive left of the recognised batters to steer us through.

Clive hadn't said much in the dressing room between innings. No one knew why he had decided to turn up. When Frankie asked if he'd been searching for us for five weeks, Clive just smiled to himself and didn't reply. There was a quiet determination about his batting today which I had seen before when Clive had a point to prove. He picked his shots carefully, placing the ball rather than belting it with all his force. But when he got a juicy half-volley outside the off-stump he lashed it through the covers with power that had the fielders gasping. It was easily the most stylish shot of the day.

No one in the team plays this shot better than Clive. Because he's a left-hander he can make room to lean into the half-volley fired across him. Notice the balance of the follow through which marks a perfectly controlled cover drive.

Wickets were falling regularly at the other end, however. Kris and Mack went in quick succession and Tylan again ran himself out by ludicrously scampering up the wicket for a nonexistent single. Ty's calling and running between the wickets were becoming a real liability.

At 66 for eight we looked dead and buried. Woofy and Ohbert were hardly likely to provide the long-term partners Clive needed to guide us to victory. But Woofy did his best. He got his head down and battled out a maiden, allowing Clive to carve a couple of boundaries in the next over. Then Brass Castle turned to their spinners and Woofy flapped at one outside the off-stump and nicked it to the keeper.

Ohbert went out to the wicket with the score on 73 – 19 runs needed to win from four overs and two balls. Perhaps the only person in the ground unaware of that was the one shuffling out to bat. Clive didn't bother to give Ohbert any instructions; he just looked firmly in his direction and determinedly clenched a fist. Ohbert waved in reply. He had two balls to face in the over and we held our breath and prayed. He attempted a sort of reverse sweep at the first and missed by a mile, but the keeper was so surprised that he let it through for a bye. Clive clipped a single from the last delivery and kept the strike.

He made good use of it. Deciding that it was too risky to rely on Ohbert to run when called, Clive set himself for boundaries. His drive over the bowler's head dissected long-on and long-off and sped on for four. He then rejected three easy singles and hammered another boundary in the air over extra-cover. However he couldn't take the single from the last ball and, with hearts in our mouths, our attention switched to Ohbert again. He missed three in a row with his bat getting further away from the ball each time. In frustration, the bowler fired in a low full toss on middle stump. Ohbert placed both pads square in front of the stumps and swung across them. Somehow he got the nick which saved him from lbw and the ball shot down to long-leg. "One," shouted Clive, but Ohbert ran two and there was nothing Clive could do about it. 86 for nine. Ohbert rushed down the pitch to the next delivery and aimed a kick at it as it passed his bat. He missed completely and there was an enormous groan from the players watching from the boundary as the keeper took the ball and removed the bails. Clive walked down the pitch and patted the disappointed number 11 on the back. "Good try, Ohbert," he said, ruefully. Even Clive knew he'd done his best. We had fallen five runs short with Clive on an unbeaten 31. We clapped Brass Castle off the pitch but our thoughts were on the League title. We'd waved farewell to that for certain.

HOME TEAM	BRASS CASTLE V GLORY GARDENS	AWAY TEAM	AT BRASS CASTLE DATE MAY 31st

INNINGS OF **BRASS CASTLE** TOSS WON BY **GG** WEATHER **Dull**

BATSMAN	RUNS SCORED	HOW OUT	BOWLER	SCORE
1 A. RASTEAU	3·1·1·2·1·4·1·2·2·2·1·4·1·4·2·1·3 2·2·2	ct ALLEN	KNIGHT	41
2 M. WATERS	2·2·2	bowled	KNIGHT	6
3 H. BRION	1·1·4	ct NAZAR	KNIGHT	6
4 N. SIMONE	2·1·1·1·4	lbw	KNIGHT	9
5 G. CHAMBERTIN	2·1	ct DAVIES	VELLACOTT	3
6 B. McGEE	2	bowled	VELLACOTT	2
7 C. GRAVE		ct SEBASTIEN	KNIGHT	0
8 T. MAHAL	2·2·3·1·1·2·1	not	out	12
9 D. MORGON	1·1·1	not	out	3
10 H. LEDBETTER				
11 B. FLEURIE				

FALL OF WICKETS											BYES	1·1·1	TOTAL EXTRAS	9
SCORE	11	20	45	65	72	74	74	8	9	10	L.BYES	1·2	TOTAL FOR	91
BAT NO	2	3	4	5	6	1	7				WIDES	1	WKTS	7
											NO BALLS	1·1		

SCORE AT A GLANCE

BOWLER	BOWLING ANALYSIS ⊙ NO BALL + WIDE													OVS	MDS	RUNS	WKT
	1	2	3	4	5	6	7	8	9	10	11	12	13				
1 H. KNIGHT	··	W·	X	·W ··	X	·W 2·	X							4	0	17	5
2 B. WOOF	1 2 2 2	X	2· 2·	X										2	0	11	0
3 C. SEBASTIEN	··	··	4·	··	4·	X								4	0	17	0
4 E. DAVIES	2·	··	··	X	3· 2·	1·	X							4	0	21	0
5 K. JOHANSEN	··	3·	··	··	X									3	0	7	0
6 T. VELLACOTT	1·2	3W·	·3·	X										3	0	12	2
7																	
8																	
9																	

HOME TEAM	BRASS CASTLE V GLORY GARDENS	AWAY TEAM	AT BRASS CASTLE DATE MAY 31st

INNINGS OF GLORY GARDENS | TOSS WON BY G.G. WEATHER Dull

BATSMAN	RUNS SCORED	HOW OUT	BOWLER	SCORE
1 C. SEBASTIEN		c & b	FLEURIE	0
2 E. DAVIES'		bowled	FLEURIE	0
3 A. NAZAR	2.2.4.1.1.2.1.2.1.2.1	ct BRION	MAHAL	19
4 H. KNIGHT	1.3.4.1.1.4.1.2.1	ct WATERS	MAHAL	18
5 C. DA COSTA	1.4.2.3.1.2.1.4.4.1.4.4	not	out	31
6 F. ALLEN	2	ct GRAVE	MORGON	2
7 K. JOHANSEN	2.1.1	lbw	LEDBETTER	4
8 T. McCURDY	4	bowled	MORGON	4
9 T. VELLACOTT	1	run	out	1
10 B. WOOF		ct McGEE	GRAVE	0
11 P. BENNETT	2	st McGEE	GRAVE	2

FALL OF WICKETS											BYES	l·l		TOTAL EXTRAS	5
SCORE	0	1	40	40	42	60	65	66	73	86	L BYES	l·l·l		TOTAL FOR WKTS	86 ALL OUT
BAT NO	2	1	3	4	6	7	8	9	10	11	WIDES				
											NO BALLS				

BOWLER	BOWLING ANALYSIS ⊙ NO BALL + WIDE													OVS	MDS	RUNS	WKT
	1	2	3	4	5	6	7	8	9	10	11	12	13				
1 B. FLEURIE	W·W	3·2	2·1	·2										4	1	17	2
2 T. MAHAL	2	·4	·4	WW·3										4	0	22	2
3 D. MORGON	W	·3	·4	·4										4	0	21	2
4 H. LEDBETTER	·2	W·4	M											3	1	10	1
5 C. GRAVE	·W·	·2												1·5	0	3	2
6 M. WATERS	4·4													1	0	8	0
7																	
8																	
9																	

Chapter Thirteen

	PLAYED	WON	LOST	POINTS
East Street Bazaar	5	4	1	40
Wyckham Wanderers	5	4	1	40
Croyland Crusaders	5	3	2	30
Glory Gardens	5	3	2	30
Arctics	5	2	3	20
Old Courtiers	5	2	3	20
Brass Castle	5	1	4	10
Stoneyheath	4	1	3	10

Cricket is full of surprises. No one had expected Wyckham Wanderers to lose their match at East Street Bazaar – but lose they did, by 20 runs, after completely collapsing against the spinners. That meant East Street went top equal with Wanderers.

"Makes no difference. We're still out of it," said Mack.

"No, we're not," said Jo. "If East Street beat Brass Castle then they win the League and there's nothing we can do. They'll be outright winners on 50 points. But if they lose and we beat Wyckham, we can still edge it."

"How?"

"If we finish on 40 with Wyckham and East Street, we win the title outright."

"I don't get it."

"It's the rules. We're equal on points but we've won both

of our games against them, so we go top."

"Fat chance of beating Wyckham with ten players," said Jacky gloomily. I didn't say anything but I felt like agreeing with him. Bad luck was sticking to Glory Gardens like a limpet. Just as we got Clive back into the side, Woofy arrived at nets and said he couldn't bowl because he had a bad back, and there wasn't much chance of him playing on Wednesday either. Matthew's finger was still too sore for batting practice, though he hoped it would be okay for the game, and Jacky could hardly walk.

"I don't mind coming second, just as long as we beat the Wanderers," said Cal. "I wouldn't want to remember the opening of our new pavilion as the day we were beaten by Liam Katz and his gang."

The new pavilion had sprung up overnight. It looked brilliant. Kiddo said it had been delivered in bits and they'd put the whole thing together on Thursday. It was white with a black roof and it had a mechanical scoreboard with a clock above it. Inside, it was nearly as big as the Eastgate Priory pavilion and the changing rooms and showers were far better.

"Not a bad effort, kiddoes," said Kiddo. "A new cricket ground and a pavilion in a couple of months from a standing start. I've got to hand it to you, and to Jo especially."

Jo blushed bright red and for once she stuck up for her big brother. "It was Francis who got us the pitch and the pavilion," she said.

Frankie laughed. "Pity it hasn't got an action replay screen and floodlights . . ." he began and then stopped abruptly as something caught his eye.

A solitary figure had appeared from behind the new pavilion. It was Marty! Everyone stared at him and he stopped dead. Eventually he spoke. "Look, I know what you're going to say, but I want to have a bowl . . . just to see if I can still do it. Anybody mind?"

Frankie threw him a ball. "I'll put my pads on, Mart – and

I'll buy you a double cheeseburger for every time you get me out."

Marty didn't even warm up. His first ball at Frankie was lightning fast and the middle stump flew out of the ground as Frankie's bat was still coming down. The next cannoned into his thigh and had him jumping and dancing like a whirling dervish. The third ball yorked him and plucked out the leg stump. Crossly, Frankie called for a new guard but, after three more deliveries had fizzed past his bat and whistled by their target, he gave up. "Someone else's turn," he said. "Clive needs the practice more than me . . . and I can't afford any more burgers."

"Two will do nicely, Frankie," said Marty. "I'll have them after Wednesday's game. I'm coming to watch you beat Wyckham."

"That's good – then it won't cost me anything. Wally's serving up all the grub on Wednesday. Whitmart are sending a barbecue and two cooks specially for the pavilion opening. If Wally thinks he can bribe me with food, he might be on the right track at last."

"Shall I ask my aunt to do some chocolate brownies?" asked Clive.

"Now I remember why I like having you in the team," said Frankie, with a greedy gleam in his eye.

Real summer arrived at last in the week of the Wyckham game and on Monday and Tuesday after school we practised in the Glory Gardens nets in warm sunshine. Marty and Clive came along on both occasions and they looked in prime form. It didn't take a genius to realise that the selection meeting for the Wyckham game was going to be a lively one. Woofy was definitely out of the reckoning, but Matthew wanted to play and so did Clive. That made 11 including Ohbert. The wild card was Marty. I knew that Erica was keen to have him back in the squad for the big game. What would Jo say to that?

The three of us met in the pavilion on Tuesday evening and

immediately Erica dropped a bombshell. "You're skipper tomorrow night, Hook," she said.

"What? I don't get it."

"Remember your promise? You can't back out."

"But why would you want to pack it in now? You've done a great job."

"I've given it a go but we shouldn't have lost that last game. You might have done better."

"I doubt it."

"So do I, really. But I'd prefer to be vice captain, if that's okay with you . . . and Marty too, I suppose."

"He's not playing," Jo said firmly.

Erica was on the point of protesting when I stepped in. "You're right Jo. We can't drop Ohbert for Marty – not after what he's done for the club."

"But . . ." Erica protested.

I knew what she was thinking. On a straight cricketing choice it would have been Marty every time. Liam Katz would be over the moon if he knew we were dropping our best and most destructive bowler for a no-hoper like Ohbert – but that wasn't the point. "If you were still captain, I'd go along with you, Erica," I said. "But you're not. And I'm voting with Jo on this one."

"Fair enough," said Erica with a faint smile.

Chapter Fourteen

If Marty was disappointed at being left out of the team he didn't show it. But both Jacky and Clive told me they weren't impressed with the selectors' choice. Even without Marty, however, the team was a strong one. Everyone felt more confident having Clive back in the side – particularly as he seemed to be coming back to something approaching his real form. And I was happier batting at six again too.

Matthew Rose	Mack McCurdy
Cal Sebastien	Frankie Allen
Azzie Nazar	Kris Johansen
Clive da Costa	Tylan Vellacott
Erica Davies	Ohbert Bennett
Hooker Knight	

Of course it wasn't that simple. Before lunch on Wednesday Tylan had to go home from school with one of his asthma attacks and Marty was put on standby as twelfth man. Jo rang Tylan's home at half past four but there was no reply, and no sign of him at the ground half an hour later either. It looked as if Marty was back in the team after all.

I didn't say a word about our last-minute selection problems to Liam Katz as we walked out to toss. The sun was blazing down and Glory Gardens rec hadn't looked better all season. A large crowd of supporters had gathered, mainly around the pavilion; the Glory Gardens fans on the left and almost as many Wyckham Wanderers followers to the right.

"Not a bad little ground you've got here," Liam said grudgingly. "The outfield looks dodgy over there though." He pointed down the slope towards the poplars and the ditch where a lone figure was seated under a huge red and yellow M.C.C. umbrella.

"It gets muddy down there sometimes," I confessed. "But it'll have dried out okay today." We approached the all-weather pitch. "It's the first time we've played on it."

"Is it quick?" asked Liam.

"Dunno. I expect it will be a good surface to bat on. I doubt anyone will get a lot of movement off the seam."

I tossed the coin and Liam called heads. It was tails and I chose to bat. First blood to Glory Gardens.

"You'll need a massive total," said Liam. "I warn you, I'm in excellent form."

I was ready for Katzy's bragging because Jo had given me a look at his scores for the season. "I heard you got a duck in your last game," I said casually.

"Well, yeah, maybe. But I had a 50 in the one before that."

"It was the spinner who got you at East Street, wasn't it?" I said, wondering how much we'd miss Tylan in this game.

Liam didn't reply. He didn't like to be reminded of his failures.

At last the game got underway. Matthew took the first strike against Win Reifer, who was bowling down the hill. We all agreed that Win was even faster than last year – which made him nearly supersonic. Even Marty would have a job matching him for pace. Win puts everything into his bowling and the result is usually fast but erratic. He'd got his sights lined up today, however, and Matthew had to play at every delivery in the first over. He got off the mark with a glance down to fine-leg for two.

Wyckham always get fired up when they play us, and Bazza

Woolf's first over produced a ludicrious appeal for a catch behind – the ball clearly came off Cal's pad. The next delivery was fired in and pitched on middle stump. Cal got well forward to it but it nipped back and hit him on the front pad. It looked as if it was going well down the leg side but there was a huge appeal again and this time the Wyckham umpire responded by slowly raising his finger.

"Look where Charlie Gale is standing. He's gone way over to leg to take that," said Mack, pointing at the Wyckham keeper.

"And Cal was a mile down the track, too," said Jacky.

"He even takes his guard a foot out of the crease," added Azzie.

No one thought he was out, but Cal made his way back to the pavilion without a moment's hesitation. He'd had an awful League season with the bat, and somehow you always get lousy umpiring decisions when things are going against you. But Cal was the last person to let that get him down; he knew he would always bounce back – probably by taking a hatful of wickets in the Wyckham innings.

Azzie drove the first ball he received for four, as if in revenge for Cal's dismissal. Then, surprisingly, Matthew got in on the scoring action too. His perfectly executed drive off the back foot bisected the covers and raced across the boundary.

"It's a bit soon for Matt to knock one off the square, isn't it?" said Frankie, sarcastically.

"Lovely shot," cried Erica, applauding Matthew energetically. Poor old Matt comes in for a lot of criticism for his slow scoring – he's a solid opener and a sticker but he can also play the shots when he wants.

The new pitch seemed to be playing well enough, although, judging from Azzie's timing, it was a bit on the slow side. He struck another glorious four over mid-off, however, and it raced down the slope to the boundary. With 18 on the board everything seemed set up for a big Azzie innings.

Matthew is a strong back-foot player because he gets up on his toes and allows his weight to come through the shot. Notice the position of the feet and the straight follow-through as he rocks on to the front foot.

"Who's that old bloke on the boundary?" said Frankie as the man under the M.C.C. umbrella jumped up, retrieved the ball, and hurled it in to the keeper. "He's got a fair throw."

"He's probably a Wyckham fan," said Jo. "I've never seen him here before. That's 18 for one. Can you put it up, Francis?"

Frankie groaned and rose to his feet to operate the new scoreboard. As he did, Azzie went for another expansive drive and edged to cover, where Liam Katz took a sharp catch low down. He leapt in the air, threw the ball up theatrically and set off on a wild lap of triumph, giving everyone in the team a big high-five as he went past. Katzy knew exactly how important Azzie's wicket was to his side.

Frankie adjusted the scoreboard. "18 for two," he said glumly.

"Last player ten," said Jo.

"When Katzy behaves in that way I feel I'd like to shake him warmly by the throat," murmured Frankie.

Clive and Matthew steadied things for Glory Gardens with some sensible cricket, taking plenty of singles, and after three overs apiece the opening pace attack came off to be replaced by Liam Katz at one end and the leggie Youz Mohamed at the other. Liam bowled an immaculate maiden to Matthew, giving Frankie plenty to moan about. But the roars and applause returned as Clive lifted the spinner over mid-on for four. Two balls later he went down the track to him again and misread the length. He missed completely and quickly slid his left foot back into the crease, but he was too late for Charlie Gale's lightning hands behind the stumps. He flicked off a single bail and Old Sid's finger shot up for the stumping.

Eight overs had gone and we were 31 for three with our two fastest run getters back in the pavilion. Erica and Matthew tried to push the scoring along but Wyckham tightened the screw. Some accurate and nagging bowling from Katz and Youz's clever flight and change of pace were a real handful on this slow pitch. The total limped to 40 but the tension grew ball by ball and finally, trying to force the pace, Erica ran herself out. It came from a brilliant direct hit – but unfortunately the cover-point fielder was Liam Katz, and we all groaned as he set off on another of his victory laps.

I joined Matthew at the wicket and defended the last two balls of Youz's over. He wasn't turning it much but his length and flight variation were tricky, and he bowls so straight that to score runs you have to take a chance of playing him across the line.

"That's 12 overs gone," I reminded Matthew. "If you can push the singles, I'll play a few shots."

Matthew obliged with a run from the first ball of Katzy's next over and then, to the huge delight of the crowd, I lifted him over mid-wicket for four. The 50 came up in the next over. Stepping back and giving myself room, I drove Youz through the covers for four. Then Matthew got in on the act with a lovely square cut for two.

Liam and Youz came to the end of their eight overs. They had conceded just 23 runs between them, and that put the pressure on us to attack from now on. To keep us on the back foot, Liam immediately reintroduced Win Reifer to bowl his final over at me.

Win's first ball whistled over my shoulder and was called a no-ball by Old Sid. I just got my bat down on the next delivery, a block-hole yorker, and squirted it down to fine-leg for two. The next was short again and screamed past the outside edge of my bat through to the keeper. Then came the off-stump half-volley. I was on it like a hawk and the sweet sound of the bat told me that I'd middled it to perfection. Liam Katz pounced in the covers, but his dive was far too late to get a hand on it. The ball had crossed the boundary before he picked himself up and he wearily trotted back to retrieve it. With three singles off the last three balls, we took ten off the over and Win slouched back to the outfield.

Liam Katz turned to his fifth bowler. It was time for out-and-out attack, but that meant taking chances. The luck didn't go our way. Another direct hit on the stumps, this time from Bazza Woolf at mid-wicket, ran Matthew out going for a second run. He'd scored 19.

Frankie joined me with a gleam in his eye. "Let me at them," he said. He pulled his second ball in the air for two, and then, with an amazing heave, planted a ball well outside off-stump over mid-wicket. He even had the nerve to rehearse the shot afterwards, as if to show his disappointment that it had gone for four rather than six. His next blow would have

111

been a certain six if he had connected but it brushed his pad and clattered into the stumps. Frankie looked back at the wreckage, shrugged, and departed.

Kris joined me with the score on 76 and three overs remaining. I reckoned that Bazza Woolf would be given the last over so we needed to make the most of the next two. The Glory Gardens bench cheered every run, but Wyckham had dropped all but two of their fielders out to the boundary and it was no easy task to find a way through. Finally, however, I stepped back, gave myself room and heaved over square cover. The ball easily beat the fielder in the deep to the boundary. Then Kris holed out at long-on with the score on 90.

Bazza began the final over. I cracked the first ball into the covers and ran a single. Mack played and missed and then managed a jumpy little dead-bat shot and dropped the ball in front of him. We raced through for another run. The next was the yorker and I just succeeded in keeping it out. Two runs off four balls; Bazza was bowling like someone possessed. The fifth ball was very fast and I stepped back and feathered it down to third-man for two. Liam adjusted the field again for the last ball and finally Bazza raced in. As I expected it was another attempted yorker and I went down the wicket to turn it into a full toss. I swung across the line. The ball took the edge and I ran hard without looking. But before I reached the other end, the cheer from the boundary told me that the snick had gone for four to long-leg. If Liam hadn't moved the fielder, it would have gone straight to him. We rounded off the innings just two short of the hundred. Jo quickly put my score up as we walked towards the pavilion. It was 37 not out.

INNINGS OF GLORY GARDENS...... TOSS WON BY G.G... WEATHER Sunny

BATSMAN	RUNS SCORED	HOW OUT	BOWLER	SCORE
1 M. ROSE	2.4.1.1.1.1.2.1.1.1.2.1	run	Out	19
2 C. SEBASTIEN		lbw	WOOLF	O
3 A. NAZAR	4.2.4	ct KATZ	WOOLF	10
4 C. DA COSTA	2.1.2.1.4	st GALE	MOHAMED	10
5 E. DAVIES	1.2	run	out	3
6 H. KNIGHT	4.1.2.2.4.1.1.3.3.1.1.2.4.1 1.2.4	not	out	37
7 F. ALLEN	2.4	bowled	HUBBARD	6
8 K. JOHANSEN	2.1.1.1	ct WOOD	HUBBARD	5
9 T. McCURDY	1	not	out	1
10 M. LEAR				
11 P. BENNETT				

FALL OF WICKETS											BYES			TOTAL EXTRAS	7
SCORE	2	18	31	41	67	76	90				L.BYES	1.1.1.1.1		TOTAL FOR	98
BAT NO	2	3	4	5	1	7	8				WIDES NO BALLS	1		WKTS	7

BOWLER	1	2	3	4	5	6	7	8	9	10	11	12	13	OVS	MDS	RUNS	WKT
1 W. REIFER	:.	4.2.	2.											4	0	21	0
2 B. WOOLF	:4 W	4 W 2	:.		2. 4.									4	0	21	2
3 L. KATZ	M	:2.	:2 4.											4	1	11	0
4 Y. MOHAMED	:4 W	:. :.	2 2											4	0	12	1
5 T. WOOD	3.. 2.2													2	0	14	0
6 S. HUBBARD	3.4 W.. W													2	0	13	2
7																	
8																	
9																	

BOWLING ANALYSIS ⊙ NO BALL + WIDE

Chapter Fifteen

Tylan arrived in the ten-minute break between innings while Kiddo was giving us a pep talk about chasing every ball and backing up all the throws. As Marty hadn't batted there was technically no reason why Tylan couldn't play but he said he was still wheezing too much. "I've just come for the food," he admitted.

The Whitmart chefs were busy getting the barbecue ready alongside the pavilion and Frankie was already showing such a healthy interest in it that I wondered whether he would be able to concentrate on his wicket-keeping.

"There's no starting until we've finished playing," he said anxiously to Tylan and Jacky, who had also come to support us. The only missing member of the squad was Woofy.

"Here are the chocolate brownies," said Clive, producing a large carrier bag which Frankie snatched from him and tore open immediately.

A puzzled expression came over his face as he plunged his hand into the bag. "What's this?" he asked, pulling out a large plucked chicken by the feet. "Clive!" he said, closely inspecting the upside-down chicken which still had its head on. "I'd say you'd committed a foul."

"Oh my God," said Clive. "I've brought the wrong bag. Give it to me . . . that's our dinner."

"Is it a Whitmart chicken?" said Frankie, inspecting the bird closely. "You never know, it might be a spy."

A few of the spectators who had gathered round to see what we were laughing at were faced by Frankie doing a strange dance with a chicken in his arms. "This is Brownie the Hen," he said to them without a smile. "She's our new mascot."

Jo gave him a sharp prod in the back and told him to go and put on his keeper's pads immediately. Frankie tossed the chicken back to Clive. "It's a funky chicken," he said, "but I'd prefer to have chocolate brownies any day."

I gave Marty the first over from the top end. He seemed quite relaxed but he had a fearsome expression on his face as he raced up to the crease and fired down his first ball. It burst through the batsman's late defensive push and bounced millimetres over middle stump. Frankie took it in front of his face and clapped his gloves together in approval. From that moment on the tension did not let up for one second.

The next ball was even quicker. It took an inside edge and evaded the stumps, Frankie, everything. It raced towards the boundary with Ohbert in hot pursuit from long-leg.

"Ten to one on the ball," said Frankie, watching Ohbert scampering along at an angle to the boundary – downhill and out of control. Suddenly we saw him kick his feet in the air and launch himself in the direction of the ball. "Oh no, please, not a sliding stop!" said Mack. But there was no going back for Ohbert. This was the wet part of the ground and he was careering downhill. He seemed to gather pace as he hit the deck and went into the slide. "Weeeeeee!" With a cry like a squealing pig, Ohbert slid ten metres, aquaplaned across the boundary, flew between the man with the M.C.C. umbrella and the line of poplars, and vanished over the bank into the ditch. For a moment the ground was silent. But Mack noticed that Ohbert had somehow managed to stop the ball just inside the boundary as he streaked past it. He raced over and returned a flat throw above the stumps to Frankie. Then, as Mack and the man with the umbrella went to investigate the damage, a mud-splattered and dripping Ohbert emerged unharmed from the ditch to uncontrollable laughter all round.

"Brilliant splashdown, Ohbert," spluttered Frankie.

"Saved two runs, too!" said Erica.

"Do you want to go and change, Ohbert?" I asked.

"Oh but . . . no, Hooker. I'll be all right," said Ohbert, resuming his fielding position as if nothing had happened. A lump of mud slid off the top of his head and ran down his face.

At last Marty raced in again and a perfect yorker flattened the opener's leg stump. That brought Liam Katz to the wicket; he has taken to batting at three these days – both for Wyckham and for the county. Liam always looks full of confidence when he comes to the wicket – as if he expects to make runs. He glanced round the field with that faintly supercilious smile.

Marty steamed in again. What had he had for tea? Rocket fuel? He bowled a snorter which went past everything – bat, stumps, keeper's gloves – and thudded into Frankie's chest. Marty followed through, standing eyeball to eyeball with Liam.

"Bowling, Marty," gasped Frankie, rubbing his chest. The smile had disappeared from Liam's face. He knew he was in a contest.

The other opener was new to us – a left-hander. Kris's standard delivery is an away-cutter to left-handers, which is why I decided to open with her from the ditch end. After Marty's express pace Kris is only just about medium, and the Wyckham player had plenty of time to play her. I could see that he liked to get on to the front foot and I asked Kris to try a couple at him short of a length. The second was too short and the left-hander pulled her for four.

Marty resumed his onslaught on Liam, who got behind everything but still received a painful-looking blow just above the thigh pad from an extra-fast lifter. Then he reminded us of his class and produced a cracking cover drive played on the

up. It came off the bat like a bullet and ⌐
get a hand to it. Liam was beaten again ⌐
then took a single from the last of the ov⌐

The question was whether to give M⌐
Katzy produced the answer for me by k⌐
the attack. He took nine runs off her sec⌐
hammered pull shot which went throug⌐
tack and decided to bowl Marty out and keep Kris back for a
couple of overs at the end of the innings.

Again Marty went past the outside edge of Katzy's bat.
Then he completely did him with a slower one, but it bounced
in front of Frankie and he let it through for two byes. Marty
responded with a fast yorker, dug out just in time by the
Wyckham captain. How he survived that over was a total
mystery, especially to Marty. After the last ball had produced
an enormous, unanswered appeal for lbw, he grabbed his
sweater from the umpire, glared at Liam and trudged down
to third-man.

Marty's action is absolutely classical. Take particular note of the "lean back" in the delivery stride to give maximum momentum. Notice also the high front knee, his sideways-on approach to the crease with the front foot landing virtually in line with the back foot, and the follow through with eyes still looking down the pitch over the bowling shoulder towards the batsman.

"That's the best you've bowled . . . ever," I said catching up with him.

"There's no justice for fast bowlers," mumbled Marty. "What does it take to get an edge?"

"Next over," I said. "You'll see." And I rushed back to set the field for Erica at the other end.

She hit the spot immediately and was unlucky not to pick up the wicket of the left-hander when he flicked across the line and the ball spooned into space on the leg side.

Marty bowled again. He now had the left-hander in his sights and bowled an express delivery just short of a length which moved back off the seam and hammered into the batter's pad, just above the knee roll. "Too high," said Old Sid, turning down the appeal.

Frankie mumbled something about Blind Pugh and settled down again to make a brilliant stop as Marty, for once, strayed down the leg side. The third ball of the over seemed to swing late and there was an audible snick. The catch wouldn't have carried to Cal in the slips if he hadn't dived forward and scooped it up brilliantly, one-handed. Old Sid looked over towards the square-leg umpire to check that it had carried, and for a horrible second it looked as if he wasn't going to give it. Then his finger went up. Marty raced over to congratulate Cal on his brilliant catch – I can just imagine what he'd have said if he had dropped it.

They were 26 for two.

Another perfect cover drive from Liam in Erica's next over was a reminder of the danger he presented. If he batted for ten overs the odds were heavily on Wyckham winning the game. I gambled on Cal to get the breakthrough by taking the pace off the ball and letting the batsmen make a mistake. This wasn't a pitch for medium pacers and I still had the nasty feeling we were going to miss Tylan badly before the end of the game.

The Wyckham plan confirmed my fears. They attacked the medium pace of Erica and just worked Cal around for singles. On this slow pitch there was so little room for error and the bad balls stood up and asked to be hit. Liam seized on another slightly over-pitched delivery and drove it through mid-off for his fourth boundary. It was time for another bowling change and I was the only front-line bowler left.

My first couple of balls were at Billy Tate, another

Wyckham left-hander. He's an awkward player to bowl at because he tends to work you on the leg side but if you give him any width outside the off-stump he'll hammer it away square. He flicked one behind square to bring Katzy on strike. My first ball to him was a tempter outside the off-stump, which he left alone. Next I fired in a good yorker and he prodded it away. I tried the away-swinger, over-pitched, and he helped himself to another boundary through the covers. The 50 came up. It had taken them one ball short of 12 overs.

Marty wandered over to have a word with me at the end of my run. "Keep it pitched-up and straight," he said.

"But then he'll hit me over the top."

"Post long-on and long-off on the boundary and give him something to aim at. Then he can either hit it down their throats or play across the line."

It was worth a try. I pushed Marty and Matthew back for the catch and bowled Liam a straight half-volley. He went for it and the ball flew in the air right between the two deep fielders. Matthew flung himself despairingly at it and it bounced in and out of his right hand. Marty covered behind him and stopped the four. "Nearly," he shouted to me. If only I'd placed Matt a little straighter.

Cal continued to do a brilliant containing job but I was now scratching my head about who to bring on after his spell. Kris had two more; Erica one. I wasn't sure either of them could handle Liam Katz in this mood. No one had so far, except Marty, and he was bowled out.

I bowled a no-ball and re-marked my run. This would be my slower ball which I bowl like an off-break to the left-hander. I concentrated my sights on the off-stump as a target and bowled. Perfect. It pitched on a length and cut into the left-hander as he checked the shot which he'd played far too early. Frankie took it behind the stumps and he and Cal went up for the catch immediately. I hadn't heard the snick but the umpire had, and Billy Tate was on his way back to the pavilion.

To fool the batter everything about the slower ball must be the same as your standard delivery – except the wrist action. I slide my fingers down the side of the ball at the point of delivery so that it comes out slower and with a higher traject-ory. And, if you're lucky, it also turns when it hits the pitch.

I did a quick calculation. There were six overs left. They needed to push up the scoring rate to seven an over – so our best tactics were to keep Liam off the strike and bottle up the batter at the other end. Unfortunately, the new player at the crease was Charlie Gale, their keeper, the last person in the world you can imagine being bottled up.

He greeted Frankie with a cheery wave. "Good catch that, Frankie," he said. "But did he hit it?"

"Did he hit it?" sneered Frankie. "Even Blind Pugh would have given that one."

"Middle please, Sid," shouted Charlie to the Wyckham umpire.

"Is your ump called Sid, too?" asked Frankie.

"Yes."

"So we've got Old Sid and Young Sid."

"But I thought yours was called Blind Pooh."

"Blind Pugh. That's his nickname."

I glared at Frankie to shut him up and bowled a straight, quick delivery at Charlie, which he edged onto his pad, and it nearly rolled back on the stumps. He got off the mark next ball from a snick down to third-man, where Ohbert fumbled and allowed them through for a couple.

Ohbert's throw finally rolled in and came to a stop at Frankie's feet. "We call him Cinderella," said Frankie to Charlie. "He's always late to the ball."

At last, in his final over, Cal got his reward. He drew Charlie Gale forward, beat him, and we watched him overbalance almost in slow motion. Behind the stumps Frankie waited and waited and, as the back foot slipped over the crease, he flicked the bails off.

"Howzat!" he snapped at Old Sid at square-leg. And the umpire smartly raised his finger.

There was a big cheer and the figure under the M.C.C. umbrella shouted something at Frankie. Charlie looked back at his stumps and laughed. "So much for Blind Pugh," he said to Frankie, as he slung his bat over his shoulder and walked off.

Liam Katz began to build a partnership with the new batsman – yet another left-hander. Kris came back at the bottom end and she was carved over the covers for four from the only bad ball in an otherwise tight over.

They needed 24 from three as I began my fourth and last. Liam advanced down the track to me and took two runs to bring up his 50. We all applauded his brilliant knock. Apart from Marty, no one had troubled him and he hadn't given us a chance throughout his innings. Of course, Liam spoilt it all by strutting ostentatiously down the pitch to exchange a high-five with the non-striker and then waved his bat frantically to milk the applause from the pavilion.

I got past him with my next ball, however. Then I dropped everyone back and bowled a yorker which he could only dig out for a single. A leg-bye brought him back on strike for my last ball. I bowled on off-stump going away and he went for the big cover drive and got a thick inside edge. It was in the air and flying over mid-off but Matthew dived and the ball slapped against the palm of his hand. He dived again and just failed to reach the rebound. It would have been a remarkable catch if only he had hung on to it. If only.

I decided to continue with Kris from the ditch end, which meant Erica would bowl the last over from the top. They needed 19 runs from the two overs and the first three balls of Kris's over yielded just a single. But then Liam chanced his arm and drove her straight back up the hill for six, just clearing Marty's athletic leap on the boundary. Now Wyckham were favourites. I pushed the field right back and Liam swung again. This time it bounced to the right of Marty and he managed to dive and stop the boundary, but they ran two.

"Keep it there," I said to Kris. "We'll get him."

"Just pray he doesn't hit another six," she said.

She bowled an identical ball and Liam's shot was again soaring in the air towards the long-on boundary. Marty got it in his sights and ran. It was dropping to his right in front of the sightscreen when he dived. Both hands wrapped round the ball and he held on as he hit the ground.

"Out!" shouted Frankie, charging down the track. All the fielders converged on Marty, who was grinning all over his face. We hardly noticed Liam making his way disconsolately back to the pavilion, but we finally joined in the applause as he left the field. No one could deny that it had been a class innings. He'd made 60.

Erica began the last over needing to stop them making eight

runs. They nudged a single, then Youz Mohamed hit her down to the mid-wicket boundary where even Clive couldn't stop them running two. Mack intercepted a blistering drive on the cover boundary and nearly got a run out as they hesitated over taking a second. Even so, an action replay would have probably given the decision to Erica as she whipped off the bails – but Young Sid gave the batter the benefit of the doubt.

Suddenly it was down to the last two balls with three to win because if the scores were level they'd win on the wicket rule. Erica risked a slower ball and it was hit straight up in the air over the bowler's head. She raced back and only just failed to get a hand on it. One run. With Youz facing the last ball I posted everyone three-quarters of the way out to the boundary – we had to stop them running two.

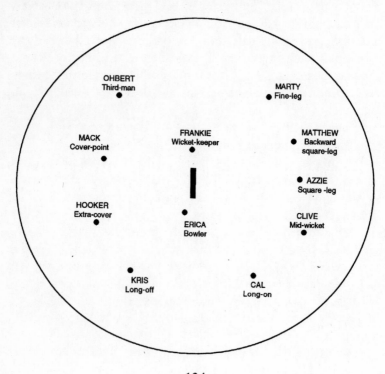

Youz took a huge swing at a good length ball and got a thick edge down to third-man . . . where Ohbert was lurking, well camouflaged in his brown-and-white clothing. Whenever you try to hide someone in the field it's inevitable that the ball goes straight to him – especially if it's Ohbert. The batters had nearly completed the first run before Ohbert made a move. Then he suddenly lurched over to his left and picked up the moving ball on the first attempt as if he was plucking a flower. The Wyckham pair started on the second run and we screamed at Ohbert to throw. Mack was the quickest thinker on the pitch and he raced to the spot halfway between Ohbert and the keeper. Ohbert threw underarm and Mack caught it, swivelled and threw hard at the wicket. The ball bounced just in front of it and smacked into the base of the middle stump just as Youz threw himself into a dive for the crease. Frankie faced the square-leg umpire and bellowed an explosive "Howzaaaaat!" His appeal turned to a roar when the finger was raised. We'd won by one run.

"Magnificent, Ohbert," shouted Mack.

"Oh but I didn't really see it, Mack," admitted our hero.

HOME TEAM	GLORY GARDENS V WYCKHAM WAND'RS	AWAY TEAM	AT GLORY GARDENS DATE JUNE 7th.

INNINGS OF WYCKHAM WANDERERS .... | TOSS WON BY G.G. ..... WEATHER Sunny

BATSMAN	RUNS SCORED	HOW OUT	BOWLER	SCORE
1 A.WOOD	2 >>	bowled	LEAR	2
2 N.CARTILEDGE	4·1	ct SEBASTIEN	LEAR	5
3 L.KATZ	4·1·2·4·3·2·4·2·1·4·1·4·1·2·1· 1·2·1·(40)·2·1·1·4·2·H·6·2 >>	ct LEAR	JOHANSEN	60
4 B.TATE	1·1·1·1·1 >>	ct ALLEN	KNIGHT	5
5 C.GALE	2·1·1 >>	st ALLEN	SEBASTIEN	4
6 S.HUBBARD	1·1·1	not	out	4
7 Y.MOHAMED	2·2·1·1 >>	run	out	6
8 T.WOOD				
9 J.BUTT				
10 W.REIFER				
11 B.WOOLF				

FALL OF WICKETS											BYES	2		TOTAL EXTRAS	11
SCORE	2	26	56	63	89	97					L.BYES	1·1·1·1·1·1·1·1		TOTAL FOR	97
	1	2	3	4	5	6	7	8	9	10	WIDES				
BAT NO	1	2	4	5	3	7					NO BALLS	1		WKTS	6

SCORE AT A GLANCE

BOWLER	BOWLING ANALYSIS ⊙ NO BALL + WIDE													OVS	MDS	RUNS	WKT
	1	2	3	4	5	6	7	8	9	10	11	12	13				
1 M.LEAR	:⊙ : : 4 M W X													4	2	7	2
2 K.JOHANSEN	: 4 2·7 X : : 1 6⊙ X													4	0	26	1
3 E.DAVIES	: 2 :⊙ 4 X :½													4	0	22	0
4 C.SEBASTIEN	: : : 2 : W X													4	0	13	1
5 H.KNIGHT	: 4⊙ : : 2 : X													4	0	19	1
6																	
7																	
8																	
9																	

Chapter Sixteen

A strange thing happened after the game. The barbecue was in full swing and there was no sign of Frankie.

Cal was so shocked that he persuaded me to help him search for him. We found him in front of the pavilion, staring up at the sky. "Are you okay?" I asked.

"Fine."

"What are you looking for?"

"Woofy," said Frankie.

"Well, you won't find him up there," said Cal, with a laugh.

"Who knows," said Frankie.

"By the way," said Cal. "Do you know that little bloke who was sitting on the boundary?"

"The one in the white hat who looked like Colonel Saunders? No, why?"

"Because I'm sure I heard him shout, 'Well done, Frankie,' when you made that stumping."

"Never seen him before in my life."

Cal shrugged. "If you don't come now, you'll miss all the food."

Frankie suddenly seemed to wake up. "Hell. I'd forgotten about that. Is there any left? I'm starving."

There was plenty. The Whitmart feast was enormous – sausages, burgers, steaks, huge prawns, chicken legs. And the real chocolate brownies had arrived too, with Clive's aunt, who had also brought a big fruitcake. Gatting was waddling expectantly round the tables, waiting to pounce like a fat brown shark on anything that dropped to the ground. Frankie loaded his plate greedily.

On the steps of the pavilion Kiddo was putting the finishing touches to assembling a very old microphone. All of a sudden he boomed, "Ladies and gentlemen, I'd like to congratulate both teams on a fine game of cricket and I want to introduce you to Jo Allen who has an important announcement to make."

Jo approached the microphone shyly and blushed. "Ahem. I just wanted to tell you that Brass Castle beat East Street Bazaar this evening by three wickets. And so Glory Gardens are League champions for the second year in succession."

There was a huge cheer from the Glory Gardens players and supporters and a groan from the Wyckham lot. Charlie Gale, Win Reifer and some of the other opposition players eventually came over to congratulate us – but I noticed Katzy kept well away. Everyone was talking at once about our unlikely triumph when Frankie leapt forward and grabbed the microphone from his sister.

"You may have been wondering where Woofy is today," he said excitedly. "Well, if you look up now you might see him."

A small plane was coming in quite low over the rec. As we watched it banked and a long banner unfurled behind it. The plane came round slowly and flew in front of the crowd. The banner read:

HANDS OFF THE PRIORY

There was a burst of spontaneous applause and we turned to listen to Frankie at the microphone again. With a flourish he opened a sheet of paper and started to sing:

Glory, glory, glory,
Listen to our song,

128

We are Glory Gardens,
You won't keep us down for long.
We've got a nice green pitch
And a new pavilion, true,
But we won't be happy
Until we get back the Priory, too.

The tune was barely recognisable because it was all on one note, but Frankie belted out the words with such conviction that the end of his song was greeted by the biggest cheer of the day.

Kiddo approached the mike once more. "Thank you Frankie. That was . . . er . . . quite amazing." Out of the corner of my eye I caught sight of Gatting tossing a brownie in the air, catching it and swallowing it in one go in case anyone should challenge him for it. Kiddo turned to us again. "Ladies and Gentlemen . . . We're here to open this splendid Glory Gardens pavilion and since there is no one here from our friends at Whitmart, I shall—"

He was interrupted by a voice from the back of the crowd. "Oh yes there is. I'm from Whitmart." A small, dapper figure with a neat white beard came forward. He was wearing a white suit and a broad-brimmed white hat.

"It's your mate from the boundary again," said Cal to Frankie.

"I'm here to represent Whitmart," he said. "My name is Walter Whitman."

"Oh but . . . it's Wally!" gasped Ohbert in amazement.

Wally Whitman walked up to the microphone and tapped it. "This is the first time I've used one of these things in 20 years," he said in a quiet but clear voice. "Today is a very important one for me. On behalf of everyone at Whitmart, I would like to declare this pavilion officially open." He raised his glass of lemonade to the audience. "Here's to League champions Glory Gardens and their new pavilion!"

As the applause died away he lifted his hand again for

quiet. "Before I go I want to say two more things. First I would like to thank Glory Gardens and Wyckham Wanderers for the most exciting game of cricket I have seen in my life. And that includes Ian Botham's match at Headingley in 1981."

"You should have seen us play Griffiths Hall at the Priory," shouted Frankie.

Wally Whitman smiled. "Thank you, Frankie. It's hard to forget the Priory when you and your friends are around. As you all know, Frankie, Ohbert and Woofy have been campaigning forcefully for some weeks to save the Priory cricket ground from development by my company."

"Too right," shouted Frankie.

Wally paused for a moment and then continued. "The decision to develop the ground was made by the executive board of my company, which has my full support. It is a good business deal. But I when I learnt that the cricket club was being evicted I was concerned. However, I believed that by paying for some of the improvements at this playing field we could overcome that problem."

"Never," said Frankie. "It'll never be anything like the Priory. And what about the other Priory teams? They can't all play here."

"Precisely," said Wally, nodding at Frankie. "That's what I learnt from you, Ohbert and Woofy. I began to understand what the break-up of the Priory club meant to you and that an all-weather pitch was no substitute for the real thing. Along the way I discovered something else too – I began to remember what it's like to be mad about cricket, as everyone who plays for Glory Gardens appears to be. I've been immensely impressed with the spirit of the club." He paused again and looked out over the playing field. "So, before I came here this evening I called a board meeting of Whitmart plc."

There was a buzz of curiosity from the audience. "I won't go into details about what we discussed," continued Wally. "It was a lively meeting but, in the end I . . . er . . . I mean we, have decided to hand the ground back to Eastgate Priory Cricket Club for a period of one hundred years."

Frankie leapt in the air with a whoop of triumph. "We've done it, Ohbert. We've won!"

"However," said Wally, raising his hand again to restrain Frankie, "our offer is subject to one very important condition."

"What's that?" demanded Frankie suspiciously.

"That from now on the Priory will be known as the Whitmart Priory Ground."

"You can call it Wally Whitman's Wonder World as long as we can play cricket on it," said a delighted Frankie.

"Then that's agreed?" said Wally, beaming.

"Agreed," said Kiddo, stepping up to shake him warmly by the hand.

We all rushed up to talk to Wally and he was soon reliving the entire match with us. His champagne moment was Ohbert's stop on the boundary, and he divided his unofficial award for player of the match between me for my 37 and Marty for his opening spell.

"Oh but, Frankie," said Ohbert suddenly. "Was Woofy really flying that plane?"

"Of course not, Ohbert," said Frankie. "It belongs to a friend of his uncle's. Woofy was the sort-of co-pilot."

"I can't wait to tell him that we've got the Priory back," said Ohbert.

"If you and Frankie jump in my car, we'll go and find him now," said Wally, who was clearly enjoying himself. Ohbert and Frankie rushed off to get their kit. "Have any of you seen the Glory Gardens' website today?" Wally asked the rest of us.

No one had.

"Then I've got news for you. An Australian team has taken up Ohbert's challenge."

"What's Ohbert's challenge?" asked Jo, just as Frankie returned. He grinned at her and began to chant:

131

There's Glory Gardens and the rest,
And we've proved that we're the best.
So if any club thinks that they can beat us,
Why not get over here and meet us.

"That's up on the website?"

"For everyone to read."

"Oh my God," sighed Jo. "We must delete it immediately."

"Too late," said Wally. "Woolagong Cricket Club is coming all the way from Australia to challenge you. They'll be here in six weeks. I can hardly wait."

FINAL RESULTS AND LEAGUE PLACINGS

Glory Gardens *beat* Wyckham Wanderers by 1 run
Brass Castle *beat* East Street Bazaar by 3 wickets
Old Courtiers *beat* Croyland Crusaders by 6 runs
Arctics *beat* Stoneyheath by 17 runs

	PLAYED	WON	LOST	POINTS
Glory Gardens	6	4	2	40
East Street Bazaar	6	4	2	40
Wyckham Wanderers	6	4	2	40
Croyland Crusaders	6	3	3	30
Arctics	6	3	3	30
Old Courtiers	6	3	3	30
Brass Castle	6	2	4	20
Stoneyheath	4	1	3	10

BATTING AVERAGES

	INNS	N/O	RUNS	S/R	H/S	AVERAGE
Clive	2	1	41	87	31*	20.50
Hooker	5	1	77	83	37*	19.25
Erica	6	2	63	65	36*	15.75
Azzie	5	0	38	92	19	7.60
Frankie	6	0	43	121	17	7.14

* Signifies 'not out'. Scoring rate (S/R) is based on the average number of runs scored per 100 balls. H/S = highest score. Minimum qualification: 30 runs.

HIGHEST INDIVIDUAL SCORES

Hooker 37* v Wyckham Wanderers
Erica 36* v Old Courtiers
Clive 31* v Brass Castle

BOWLING AVERAGES

	OVERS	MDNS	RUNS	WKTS	ECON	S/R	AVERAGE
Jacky	13	1	34	10	2.8	7.8	3.4
Tylan	9	0	42	7	4.7	7.7	6.0
Hooker	15	1	56	9	4.7	10.0	6.2
Woofy	6	0	24	3	4.0	12.0	8.0
Kris	15	2	45	5	3.0	18.0	9.0
Cal	14.1	1	41	4	2.9	21.3	10.3
Marty	10	2	39	3	3.9	20.0	13.0

Strike rate (S/R) is the average number of balls bowled to take each wicket. Economy rate (ECON) is the average number of runs given away each over. Minimum qualification: 3 wickets.

BEST BOWLING

Hooker 5 for 17 v Brass Castle
Jacky 4 for 5 v Arctics
Jacky 3 for 6 v East Street Bazaar

CATCHES

	CAUGHT	DROPPED	TOTAL
Frankie	9	3	+6
Azzie	3	1	+2
Cal	3	1	+2
Erica	2	0	+2
Hooker	1	0	+1
Mack	1	0	+1
Kris	1	1	–
Marty	1	1	–
Ohbert	1	1	–
Tylan	1	2	-1
Jacky	0	1	-1
Matthew	0	2	-2

THE CRICKET PITCH

crease At each end of the wicket the crease is marked out in white paint like this:

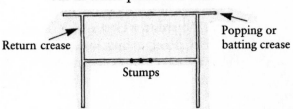

Return crease

Popping or batting crease

Stumps

The batsman is 'in his ground' when his bat or either foot are behind the batting or 'popping' crease. He can only be given out 'stumped' or 'run out' if he is outside the crease.

The bowler must not put his front foot down beyond the popping crease when he bowls. And his back foot must be inside the return crease. If he breaks these rules the umpire will call a 'no-ball'.

leg side/ off-side The cricket pitch is divided down the middle. Everything on the side of the batsman's legs is called the 'leg side' or 'on side' and the other side is called the 'off-side'.

Remember, when a left-handed bat is batting, his legs are on the other side. So leg side and off-side switch round.

leg stump Three stumps and two bails make up each wicket. The 'leg stump' is on the same side as the batsman's legs. Next to it is the 'middle stump' and then the 'off-stump'.

off/on side	See **leg side**
off-stump	See **leg stump**
pitch	The 'pitch' is the area between the two wickets. It is 22 yards long from wicket to wicket (although it's usually 20 yards for Under 11s and 21 yards for Under 13s). The grass on the pitch is closely mown and rolled flat. Just to make things confusing, sometimes the whole ground is called a 'cricket pitch'.
square	The area in the centre of the ground where the strips are.
strip	Another name for the pitch. They are called strips because there are several pitches side by side on the square. A different one is used for each match.
track	Another name for the pitch or strip.
wicket	'Wicket' means two things, so it can sometimes confuse people. 1 The stumps and bails at each end of the pitch. The batsman defends his wicket. 2 The pitch itself. So you can talk about a hard wicket or a turning wicket (if it's taking spin).

BATTING

attacking strokes	The 'attacking strokes' in cricket all have names. There are forward strokes (played off the front foot) and backward strokes (played

off the front foot). The drawing shows where the different strokes are played around the wicket.

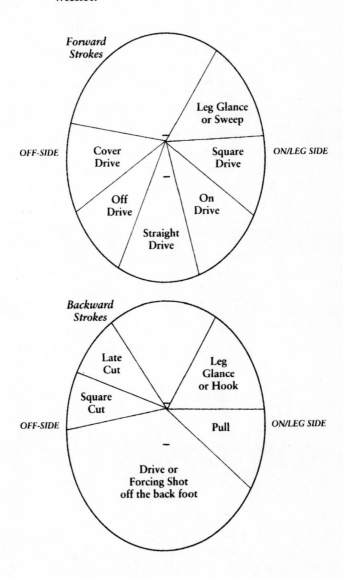

Forward Strokes

OFF-SIDE

ON/LEG SIDE

Leg Glance or Sweep

Cover Drive

Square Drive

Off Drive

On Drive

Straight Drive

Backward Strokes

OFF-SIDE

ON/LEG SIDE

Late Cut

Leg Glance or Hook

Square Cut

Pull

Drive or Forcing Shot off the back foot

backing up

As the bowler bowls, the non-striking batsman should start moving down the wicket to be ready to run a quick single. This is called 'backing up'.

bye

If the ball goes past the bat and the keeper misses it, the batsmen can run a 'bye'. If it hits the batsman's pad or any part of his body (apart from his glove), the run is called a 'leg-bye'. Byes and leg-byes are put in the 'Extras' column in the scorebook. They are not credited to the batsman or scored against the bowler's analysis.

This is how an umpire will signal a bye and leg-bye.

Bye

Leg-bye

cart	To hit a ball a very long way.
centre	See **guard**
cow shot	When the batsman swings across the line of a delivery, aiming towards mid-wicket, it is often called a 'cow shot'.
cross bat	A shot made with the bat not straight – as in the cow shot.
defensive strokes	There are basically two defensive shots: the 'forward defensive', played off the front foot and the 'backward defensive' played off the back foot.
duck	When a batsman is out before scoring any runs it's called a 'duck'. If he's out first ball for nought it's a 'golden duck'.
gate	If a batsman is bowled after the ball has passed between his bat and pads it is sometimes described as being bowled 'through the gate'.
guard	When you go in to bat the first thing you do is 'take your guard'. You hold your bat sideways in front of the stumps and ask the umpire to give you a 'guard'. He'll show you which way to move the bat until it's in the right position. The usual guards are 'leg stump' (sometimes called 'one leg'); 'middle and leg' ('two leg') and 'centre' or 'middle'.

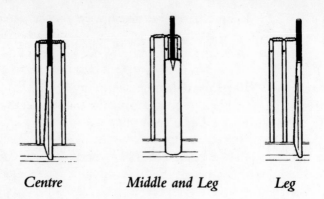

| Centre | Middle and Leg | Leg |

handled the ball   Deliberate handling of the ball while in play is one of the 10 ways of being given out.

hit the ball twice   Another strange reason for dismissal. You can use your bat to stop the ball running on to the stumps after you've played a shot, but you must not strike the ball a second time to score runs or impede the fielders.

hit wicket   If the batsman knocks off a bail with his bat or any part of his body when the ball is in play, he is out 'hit wicket'.

innings   This means a batsman's stay at the wicket. 'It was the best *innings* I'd seen Azzie play.'
But it can also mean the batting score of the whole team. 'In their first *innings* England scored 360.'

king pair   If a batter is out first ball in both innings he is said to have a 'king pair'.

knock   Another word for a batsman's innings.

lbw	Means leg before wicket. In fact a batsman can be given out lbw if the ball hits any part of his body and the umpire thinks it would have hit the stumps. There are two important extra things to remember about lbw: 1 If the ball pitches outside the leg stump and hits the batsman's pads it's not out – even if the ball would have hit the stumps. 2 If the ball pitches outside the off-stump and hits the pad outside the line, it's not out if the batsman is playing a shot. If he's not playing a shot he can still be given out.
leg-bye	See **bye**
middle/ *middle and leg*	See **guard**
out	There are six common ways of a batsman being given 'out' in cricket: bowled, caught, lbw, hit wicket, run out and stumped. Then there are a few rare ones like handled the ball and hit the ball twice. When the fielding side thinks the batsman is out they must appeal (usually a shout of 'Howzat'). If the umpire considers the batsman is out, he will signal 'out' like this:

play	You 'play forward' by moving your front foot
forward/back	down the wicket towards the bowler as you

You 'play forward' by moving your front foot down the wicket towards the bowler as you play the ball. You 'play back' by putting your weight on the back foot and leaning towards the stumps.

You play forward to well-pitched-up bowling and back to short-pitched bowling.

rabbit   Poor or tail-end batsman.

run   A 'run' is scored when the batsman hits the ball and runs the length of the pitch. If he fails to reach the popping crease before the ball is thrown in and the bails are taken off, he is 'run out'. Four runs are scored when the ball is hit across the boundary. Six runs are scored when it crosses the boundary without bouncing. This is how the umpire signals 'four':

This is how the umpire signals 'six':

If the batsman does not put his bat down inside the popping crease at the end of a run before setting off on another run, the umpire will signal 'one short' like this.

A run is then deducted from the total by the scorer.

stance The 'stance' is the way a batsman stands and holds his bat when he is waiting to receive a delivery. There are many different types of stance. For instance, side on, with the shoulder pointing down the wicket; square on, with the body turned towards the bowler; bat raised, and so on.

striker The batsman who is receiving the bowling. The batsman at the other end is called the non-striker.

stumped If you play and miss and the wicket-keeper knocks a bail off with the ball in his hands, you will be out 'stumped' if you are out of your crease.

timed out A batter will be given out if he deliberately or wilfully takes more than two minutes to come in from the moment the wicket falls.

ton A century. One hundred runs scored by a batsman.

BOWLING

arm ball A variation by the off-spinner (or left-arm spinner) which swings in the air in the opposite direction to the normal spin, i.e. away from the right-handed batsman in the case of the off-spinner.

beamer See **full toss**.

block hole A ball bowled at yorker length is said to pitch in the 'block hole' – i.e. the place where the batsman marks his guard and rests his bat on the ground when receiving.

bouncer The bowler pitches the ball very short and

bowls it hard into the ground to get extra bounce and surprise the batsman. The ball will often reach the batsman at shoulder height or above. But you have to be a fast bowler to bowl a good bouncer. A slow bouncer is often called a 'long hop' and is easy to pull or cut for four.

chinaman   A left-arm bowler who bowls with the normal leg-break action will deliver an off-break to the right-handed batsman. This is often called a 'chinaman'.

dead ball   The ball ceases to be dead from the moment the bowler starts his run. However if the bowler fails to deliver the ball, the umpire will signal 'dead ball'. After the ball has been bowled it becomes dead again when it is back in the hands of the bowler or the keeper or has crossed the boundary.

donkey drop   A ball bowled very high in the air.

dot ball   A ball from which the batsman does not score a run. It is called this because it goes down as a dot in the scorebook.

flipper   A variation on the leg break. It is bowled from beneath the wrist, squeezed out of the fingers, and it skids off the pitch and goes straight through. It shouldn't be attempted by young cricketers because it puts a lot of strain on the wrist and arm ligaments.

full toss   A ball which doesn't bounce before reaching the batsman is a 'full toss'. Normally it's easy to score off a full toss, so it's considered a bad ball. A high full toss from a fast bowler is called a 'beamer'. It is very dangerous and should never be bowled deliberately.

googly A 'googly' is an off-break bowled with a leg-break action (see **leg break**) out of the back of the hand like this.

grubber A ball which hardly bounces – it pitches and shoots through very low, usually after hitting a bump or crack in the pitch. Sometimes also called a shooter.

hat trick Three wickets from three consecutive balls by one bowler. They don't have to be in the same over i.e. two wickets from the last two balls of one over and one from the first of the next.

half-volley See **length**

leg break/
off-break The 'leg break' is a delivery from a spinner which turns from leg to off. An 'off-break' turns from off to leg.
That's easy to remember when it's a right-hand bowler bowling to a right-hand batsman. But when a right-arm, off-break bowler

bowls to a left-handed bat he is bowling leg-breaks. And a left-hander bowling with an off-break action bowls leg breaks to a right-hander. It takes some working out – but the drawing helps.

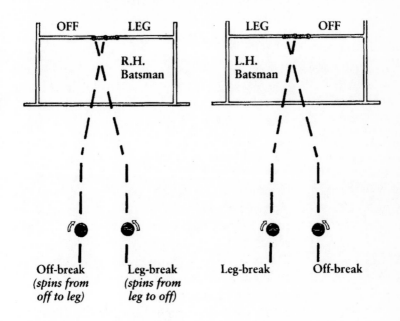

Off-break
*(spins from
off to leg)*

Leg-break
*(spins from
leg to off)*

Leg-break

Off-break

leg-cutter/ *off-cutter*	A ball which cuts away off the pitch from leg to off is a 'leg-cutter'. The 'off-cutter' goes from off to leg. Both these deliveries are bowled by fast or medium-pace bowlers. See **seam bowling**.
leggie	Slang for a leg-spin bowler.
length	You talk about the 'length' or 'pitch' of a ball bowled. A good-length ball is one that makes the batsman unsure whether to play back or

forward. A short-of-a-length ball pitches slightly closer to the bowler than a good length. A very short-pitched ball is called a 'long hop'. A 'half-volley' is an over-pitched ball which bounces just in front of the batsman and is easy to drive.

long hop   A ball which pitches very short. See **length**.

maiden over   If a bowler bowls an over without a single run being scored off the bat, it's called a 'maiden over'. It's still a maiden if there are byes or leg-byes but not if the bowler gives away a wide.

no-ball   'No-ball' can be called for many reasons.
1 The most common is when the bowler's front foot goes over the popping crease at the moment of delivery. It is also a no-ball if he steps on or outside the return crease. See **crease**.
2 If the bowler throws the ball instead of bowling it. If the arm is straightened during the bowling action it is a throw.
3 If the bowler changes from bowling over the wicket to round the wicket (or vice-versa) without telling the umpire.
4 If there are more than two fielders behind square on the leg side. (There are other fielding regulations with the limited overs game. For instance, the number of players who have to be within the circle.)
A batsman can't be out off a no-ball, except run out. A penalty of one run (an experiment of two runs is being tried in county cricket) is added to the score and an extra ball must be bowled in the over. The umpire shouts

'no-ball' and signals like this:

over the wicket If a right-arm bowler delivers the ball from the right of the stumps (as seen by the batsman) i.e. with his bowling arm closest to the stumps, then he is bowling 'over the wicket'. If he bowls from the other side of the stumps, he is bowling 'round the wicket'.

pace The 'pace' of the ball is the speed it is bowled at. A fast or pace bowler like Darren Gough can bowl at speeds of up to 90 miles an hour. The different speeds of bowlers range from fast through medium to slow with in-between speeds like fast-medium and medium-fast (fast-medium is the faster).

pitch See **length**.

round the wicket See **over the wicket**.

seam The 'seam' is the sewn, raised ridge which runs round a cricket ball.

seam bowling   Bowling – usually medium to fast – where the ball cuts into or away from the batsman off the seam.

shooter   See **grubber**.

spell   A 'spell' of bowling is the number of overs bowled in succession by a bowler. So if a bowler bowls six overs before being replaced by another bowler, he has bowled a spell of six overs.

swing bowling   A cricket ball can be bowled to swing through the air. It has to be bowled in a particular way to achieve this and one side of the ball must be polished and shiny, which is why you always see fast bowlers shining the ball. An 'in-swinger' swings into the batsman's legs from the off-side. An 'out-swinger' swings away towards the slips.

trundler   A steady, medium-pace bowler who is not particularly good.

turn   Another word for spin. You can say 'the ball turned a long way' or 'it spun a long way'.

wicket maiden   An over when no run is scored off the bat and the bowler takes one wicket or more.

wide   If the ball is bowled too far down the leg side or the off-side for the batsman to reach (usually the edge of the return crease is the line umpires look for) it is called a 'wide'. One run is added to the score and an extra ball is bowled in the over.

In limited overs cricket, wides are given for balls closer to the stumps – any ball bowled down the leg side risks being called a wide in this sort of 'one-day' cricket.

This is how an umpire signals a wide.

yorker   A ball, usually a fast one, bowled to bounce precisely under the batsman's bat. The most dangerous yorker is fired in fast towards the batsman's legs to hit leg stump.

FIELDING

backing up   A fielder backs up a throw to the wicket-keeper or bowler by making sure it doesn't go for overthrows. So when a throw comes in to the keeper, a fielder is positioned behind him to cover him if he misses it. Not to be confused with a batsman backing up.

chance   A catchable ball. So to miss a 'chance' is the same as to drop a catch.

close/deep   Fielders are either placed 'close' to the wicket (near the batsman) or in the 'deep' or 'out-field' (near the boundary).

cow corner   The area between the deep mid-wicket and long-on boundaries where a cow shot is hit to.

dolly   An easy catch.

hole-out   A slang expression for a batsman being caught. 'He holed out at mid-on.'

overthrow   If the ball is thrown to the keeper or the bowler's end and is misfielded allowing the batsmen to take extra runs, these are called 'overthrows'.

silly   A fielding position very close to the batsman and in front of the wicket e.g. silly mid-on.

sledging   Using abusive language and swearing at a batsman to put him off. A slang expression – first used in Australia.

square   Fielders 'square' of the wicket are on a line with the batsman on either side of the wicket. If they are fielding further back from this line, they are 'behind square' or 'backward of square'; if they are fielding in front of the line i.e. closer to the bowler, they are 'in front of square' or 'forward of square'.

standing up/ standing back   The wicket-keeper 'stands up' to the stumps for slow bowlers. This means he takes his position immediately behind the stumps. For fast bowlers he stands well back – often several yards away for very quick bowlers. He may either stand up or back for medium-pace bowlers.

colts

County colts teams are selected from the best young cricketers in the county at all ages from Under 11 to Under 17. Junior league cricket is usually run by the County Colts Association.

under 11s/
12s etc.

You qualify for an Under 11 team if you are 11 or under on September 1st prior to the cricket season. So if you're 12, but you were 11 on September 1st last year, you can play for the Under 11s.

FIELDING POSITIONS

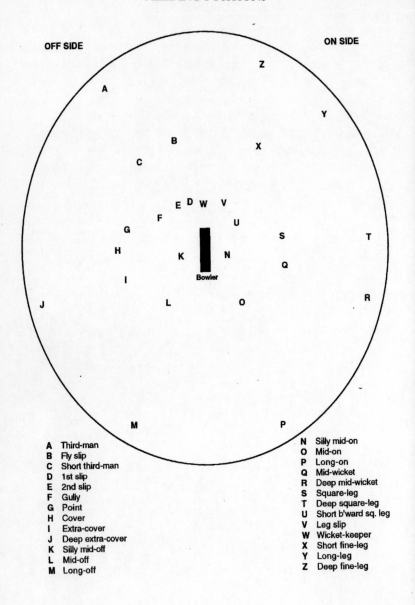

OFF SIDE

ON SIDE

Bowler

A	Third-man	**N**	Silly mid-on
B	Fly slip	**O**	Mid-on
C	Short third-man	**P**	Long-on
D	1st slip	**Q**	Mid-wicket
E	2nd slip	**R**	Deep mid-wicket
F	Gully	**S**	Square-leg
G	Point	**T**	Deep square-leg
H	Cover	**U**	Short b'ward sq. leg
I	Extra-cover	**V**	Leg slip
J	Deep extra-cover	**W**	Wicket-keeper
K	Silly mid-off	**X**	Short fine-leg
L	Mid-off	**Y**	Long-leg
M	Long-off	**Z**	Deep fine-leg

154

GLORY GARDENS

The BIG TEST

It really doesn't look like being Hooker's
season. Not only does he spend the first match
of the league suffering a dropped-catch jinx but now
there's civil war in the team over the selections.
Sometimes captaining the GLORY GARDENS Cricket
Team isn't the fun you might think. It's not the
matches that prove the most trouble for poor
Hooker – it's the infighting. He has one solution that
might work. But making Ohbert captain in his place?
That's not strategy – that's suicide.

ISBN 0-09-946131-5   **RED FOX**   £ 4.99

GLORY GARDENS

World Cup FEVER

GLORY GARDENS C.C. can't resist a challenge
and this time they're going for gold in a World Cup
competition! With teams from Barbados and South Africa
visiting the area at the same time, it's a brilliant
opportunity for the club to make its mark worldwide.
It's not long before the thrills and spills of cricket spark
off sporting drama, temper tantrums and practical jokes.
So, as Australia do battle with the West Indies and
South Africa face India, can Glory Gardens rise above
the squabbling and bring glory for England...?

ISBN 0-09-946141-2   **RED FOX**   £ 4.99

You'll be stumped without them!

GLORY GARDENS

League of CHAMPIONS

GLORY GARDENS C.C. are back and this time the stakes are high as they play to win in the League of Champions! Hooker and co have got to get their act together fast if they're going to make it through the early rounds to the final of the knock-out competition. And let's face it, with Ohbert on the team it's not as straightforward as it might seem. As the competition progresses, the pressure builds and the team realise they are going to have to pull out all the stops if they want to make it all the way to the top... and Edgbaston!

ISBN 0-09-972401-4   **RED FOX**   £ 4.99

You'll be stumped without them!

GLORY GARDENS

The Glory ASHES

• • • • • • • • • • • • •

When Ohbert creates a GLORY GARDENS website,
unknown to everyone else, his mission is to make them
the most famous junior club in the world! His claims for
the club get bigger and bigger until one day he puts out
a challenge for anyone to come and beat the 'reigning
world champions' – and the top young club in Australia
approach them to do just that. A tournament is arranged,
but when the press pick up on the story, there is much
more at stake than just their reputation…

• • • • • • • • • • • • •

ISBN 0-09-940904-6   **RED FOX**   £ 4.99

You'll be stumped without them!